T0127711

GM & GS PRIVATE INVESTIGATION SERVICE

BOOK IV

D. H. Crosby

authorHOUSE®

AuthorHouse™
1663 Liberty Drive
Bloomington, IN 47403
www.authorhouse.com
Phone: 1 (800) 839-8640

Published by AuthorHouse 02/24/2018

ISBN: 978-1-5462-3054-0 (sc)
ISBN: 978-1-5462-3053-3 (e)

Print information available on the last page.

Special thanks to

Wendy Crosby
Maggie Thornton
Linda Sims
Lynn Creech
Laurie Andrews
Wendy Ducasse

For your support!

PART FOURTEEN

CHAPTER ONE

Eunice said, "I'll just go check on the boys." She left the table.

"She did know that we were joking?" Trevor asked looking around. "I must be more tired than I thought. I am going to nap for awhile Madeline. Don't let anyone go into town."

Trevor had been up most of the night preparing for the mass media and the statements that he was going to make on behalf of the family.

Madeline looked at Marcus Buchanan, the billionaire who was puzzled by Eunice's quick retreat. He was staying at Southfork with Trevor and Madeline Porter due to the threat on their lives, and his daughter Adriana's life.

Eunice had attracted his eye at the law office where he had signed papers for a large hotel and casino to be built in this small town in North Carolina.

He had dinner with Eunice and the Porters when the explosion happened and she almost got killed.

Madeline reminded him, "She is just emotional Marcus. Remember that monster Chris Shackleford grabbed her around the neck. Thank God, Trevor's friend Lonestar was here. If he had missed and not taken him out, he could have pulled that bomb cord and blown her up. Probably would have taken us all out in the restaurant, too. So be patient, my friend, she is a good woman and worth the wait."

"Coming from you that is high praise. I have only known her for a short time, but she is special. I have not chosen well in my past relationships as you know. This is the first time a woman has turned me down. Truthfully, it is just what I needed."

Eunice spoke to Jason her thirteen year old that was addicted to action games. He and his brother Corey who had just graduated from high school last week were in a competition in the war game on the XBOX.

"Awww mom, please tell me we don't have to go home? I love this game room," Jason begged.

Corey shrugged his shoulders, "We may need an army to get him out of here Mom." He was enjoying the family being together. This game room had taken their minds off the horrible thought that their mom could have been killed yesterday.

They stopped playing and hugged her especially tight today.

"No, boys we can't go home for a couple more days. Mr. Trevor has given me orders for us all to stay here. His security men are on the job, and I feel safe. How about you two, are you good with that?" Eunice looked at her boys with love in her eyes.

She had lost her husband seven years ago and her teenage daughter, Coraine last year. She couldn't make it, if anything happened to her boys.

"That is great! Yes! Yes! No school. Right?" Jason asked.

"You didn't have but a couple more days anyway, Jason," Corey said throwing him a punch on his arm.

"You don't ever have to go to school again Corey. I've got five more years. I have to pace myself," Jason said straightening to his tallest tiptoe height. He liked to measure himself to Corey.

"We are fine, MOM. I'll keep him under control," he put his kid brother in a headlock and marched him back to the game. As she was walking to her room, she heard her boys laughing. That was music to her ears, and she wept.

Cassie her best friend had packed her suitcase for her and she had all her new clothes that she had purchased last week. She still could not believe she had shopped for herself.

She took out a white pair of slacks and donned a sleeveless shirt of navy blue. She had red high heels, but they were for work. She put her sandals on. They were more practical.

She looked in the oval mirror, the outfit was comfortable and not too fancy. It being new made it look fresh and made her feel good. She wanted to look nice for Marcus. Even though this was just one of his flings. She was going to enjoy it while it lasted.

Marcus met her in the hallway, "Don't you look gorgeous!"

"Why thank you kind sir." He had taken her hand and ask, if they could walk out by the swimming pool. The massive seating area had everything at the bar that he liked and the cooking area was fully stocked with sodas and juices.

He asked if she wanted a martini, and she shook her head.

"I'm one of the rare breed that doesn't drink. Of course, last night I probably would have said yes, but I'm fine today. I have the boys to think about. They have never seen me drink. Thank you anyways. I am just running on. It must be the caffeine. It makes me a chatterbox."

Eunice went and got a ginger ale and poured it over ice. They sat on the same glider looking at the mountains, and the beautiful view of the lake.

"You have met my daughter. She lives at the top of this mountain. I am a grandpa," Marcus laughed. He had seven others, but he didn't want to talk about his three failed marriages. All to debutantes and gold-diggers, he lamented. She would find out soon enough.

"Yes, she is a darling girl and one smart lawyer. You know she defended my Tate and Debbie. It was awful. Get her to tell you, and about my daughter's death. I cannot talk about it today or any other day without crying. This sunny day will not be spoiled on yesterdays," and she smiled at him.

"Madeline is Trevor okay?" Eunice asked.

"He is snoring like a log and he will be mad, if I don't wake him soon. Just thirty more minutes and I will wake the grizzly bear," she took a sip of her Pepsi and sat opposite them folding her long legs under her.

Eunice and Marcus had short legs and both looked at the way their feet were barely touching the ground. He looked at her feet and grinned. He was five foot three and she was a dainty five foot two.

Madeline and Trevor were tall Texans. She in heels a good six foot and Trevor towered her at six foot four.

Marcus had always had a tall beautiful woman on his arm. Now he is thinking "that was my ego" and now I am looking at a woman that is my size and definitely beautiful. "Sip your drink before you make a fool out of yourself," he said to himself.

Corey didn't know they were on the veranda and he was talking to his girlfriend on his cell phone with his back to them. "I love you too! No I cannot see you for a couple more days. I miss you too! We will make up for it! I promise!" then he turned and saw his Mom. He blushed and quickly walked inside and continuing to talk.

"Yep, young love! Ain't it grand!" Marcus was feeling his second martini. His eyes were twinkling.

Trevor came out yawning, "Mature love is better!" and kissed Madeline's ponytail and sat cuddling her up to him.

"I guess you are needing a cup of coffee so you can wake up real good, before I have to slap you," Madeline said. She got up to fix a fresh pot and he popped her on her rear.

"Behave ... we have company!" she said.

"I am going in and get the coffee. I thought I would see if the boys wanted to go swimming. Is that okay Eunice?" Madeline asked.

"They would love it. They both swim like fish or frogs," she laughed. "I can't swim so whomever can swim, please be the designated lifeguard."

Tate and Debbie came out. Tate said, "I'll watch them. Debbie and I, both can swim." He looked into her eyes remembering their first swim here. She shivered and he hugged her in the sunshine. It still had an effect on them.

Roscoe and Guy rounded the corner and Madeline said,

"Please don't tell me more bad news. I don't want to hear it."

She handed Trevor his coffee and looked at her 'boys'.

Roscoe said, “GM ... we are not going to sugar coat it,” he paused and took a deep breath. “We want a party!” then smiled at his brother, Guy.

“I don’t want anyone, but family. We won’t go off the property. We promise. What do you think?” Roscoe asked.

“Where are your wives and the kids? You must bring them every time. I am going through withdrawals not having them here,” Madeline said.

Bruce and Jana came out, “Here! Here!” they all did their cheer. “I just called Unitus. He and Adriana, and little Angel are on their way!”

Marcus was smiling, “Here! Here!” He had got use to this wonderful group of people and wanted to fit in. With his daughter, he had not been there for Adriana’s parties because he was too busy wheeling and dealing. Money was his only party. He frowned, and really regretted that now.

“There’s my Angel!” He took his granddaughter from Adriana. Unitus was eyeing Marcus and said to Adriana, “Are you sure he is okay? The man is slurring his words, dear! You won’t let me drink and hold her?”

Adriana said, “You can’t drink! You have to drive. He has for years without a problem. If you’re going to pout, I will sit beside him,” and she sat on one side of Marcus and Eunice on the other.

Trevor waved to Roscoe and Guy, and they followed him into the den. “You cannot leave the women and children at home anymore. Remember that this is not over. Jung’s men are out there.”

They went flying out the doors and raced home. One house on either side of the lake. Roscoe looked at Guy who was panting, “Your big idea was to walk to see GM.”

"I can run faster than you. You are just jealous because I can beat you. You nut! You almost tripped me," Guy said.

"I know, but I gotta walk. If I have a heart attack, who's going to take care of my four kids?" Roscoe sputtered.

"I am," Guy said walking slower. "What in the world are we going to do? Trevor is right. Soon as this media frenzy leaves town, it will not be safe for us."

"I know, Bro. We got to go and live on an island where nobody knows our name. Later GS!" Roscoe was at his entrance and he watched Guy running to get to his house's entrance.

"Beatrice we got to stay at GM again, and the housekeeper and nanny can come this time. I am making sure of that! It is no way to sugar coat it, honey!" He was packing as he spoke.

"The man that hired Chris Shackleford might ... The man is definitely going to hire someone else, and Trevor wants us all at his compound that has Federal protection," Roscoe stated.

Beatrice was throwing things into suitcases and the nanny said, "Do you want me to help?"

"No, just take care of my four babies, and I will talk to you when I get through," The nanny had tried to explain to the new housekeeper .

They had hired Mrs W which stood for Wadsworth especially picked out by Kyleigh with the same MO which equaled "old." Beatrice had given her directions to Madeline's, when she was hired.

"That's grandma's house!" and she gave her VERY few, but some details about their situation.

Otherwise, Mrs W probably would have not taken this job. The billionaire brother-in-law, Guy was paying for this treat. It had taken her best friend Kyleigh, Guy's wife to convince her to accept the help. Now she couldn't live without it, nor could Roscoe.

"We have two bedrooms, one has 4 cribs in it, and all the amenities. If you want to stay with us, I will make arrangements and you can help with the housework which we all do pitch in... Or you can go and come your regular hours. Just let me know what you decide, Mrs W," Beatrice stated.

Roscoe had all in the car by now since they had done this before, it didn't take as long. Then they were off, "over the hills and through the woods to grandma' s house we go."

Roscoe loved to sing that song. It calmed the twin girls. They were quiet. The twin boys were two years and eight months old. They were into everything even in the car seats pulling stuff out, and throwing it.

At Guy and Kyleigh's house, they were not doing well.

Kyleigh shouted, "What do you mean it is NOT over?"

"We have to go to GM's now Kyleigh! Let us pack while Madison is taking his nap," Guy said.

She came around the couch and shook him, "You got to tell me all!" Kyleigh was pacing and holding her head. "I am having a meltdown here. You had better get me to the doctor." He knew she was doing so good the first go round.

He immediately went and called her psychiatrist and scheduled her an appointment. The constant stress kept causing flashbacks. "Tomorrow at two and he ordered you some sleeping pills. I will swing by later and get them." He tried to kiss her, but she avoided the contact and stated, "If

I am in danger, then you are in danger. You are staying with Madison and me at GM's."

"Yes, Ma'am, that means you still love me," Guy had the sad puppy dog eyes working. She gave in and kissed him.

"I can't go to grandma's like this," rubbing her against his manhood.

"No you can't. Let me go get a frying pan and I'll flatten it!"

Kyleigh said. Patting her right foot as if to say, try me. He flew to the car and loaded the suitcase and fave toys. Then they were over the hills and through the woods less than a mile. He jumped out, "All gone."

Fear could make a person violent, he had witnessed her anger when in therapy. The kidnapping and brutality that she had suffered could rise at any time.

Kyleigh had fear in her eyes again. It was not going to be easy this time. He must request GM to help him tell her the severity. Jung was Jared Banks 's boss. The monster that had kidnapped her. He stopped when she was inside the house, and put both his hands over his face.

Roscoe ran to him, "What is it?" Guy said, "She is freaking out and I haven't given her any details. Beatrice has to be with her at all times, if I'm not." They took the luggage inside.

Everyone met them and they all hugged. "Long time no see! Was it just three days ago? I believe it was," said Adriana who hugged Beatrice and Kyleigh.

"We are the wives of men that love and protect their women and children," Adriana said and they held their glasses up and in unison said, "Here! Here!"

Her father, Marcus was so proud of Adriana. Eunice was holding the granddaughter Angel, and cooing to her while Unitus smiled standing beside his wife.

Eunice's boys were still playing games with the twin boys.

Tate was helping Debbie with supper as was Beatrice's housekeeper, and Madeline.

Trevor saw his wife Madeline beaming again. He kissed her ponytail and said, "You do love a full house. Guy says he needs you to help with Kyleigh, she's not doing well. Just the word Jung will destroy her recovery."

GM took Kyleigh to her bedroom, "How are you doing? This is just another temporary stay. I love having you and it means you will be safe. You have always been safe with me."

"That is true and I love visiting … but Guy is keeping something from me and I know it. It's something bad that he does not want me to know. That makes me mad," Kyleigh was tearful.

She hugged GM like she did when she was a little girl, her mother never hugged her. GM had practically raised her. She trusted Madeline. "Tell me?"

"We do not want any of the family away from here because Trevor thinks the man Jung that hired Chris may hire someone else. So he wants Lonestar to take him out. He will Kyleigh or one of the Feds will. They have several snipers also. We just have to sit pat, and wait." Looking into Kyleigh eyes, "Do you understand?"

"Yes, now I know. Why couldn't Guy tell me?" tilting her head to the side asking for an answer.

"He loves you and he doesn't want to say anything to you that will cause you pain, my dear. It's that simple."

"I will forgive him then, when you put it that way," and they hugged again. After blowing her nose, Kyleigh stood and they walked back into the living room.

There Guy was bouncing Madison, a rowdy two year and eight month old cousin of Roscoe and Beatrice's Cain and Caleb. They all wanted down. Roscoe had one under each arm and they were kicking.

It did not phase Roscoe. They were going to sit and eat first, then they could play. He won that round, the boys were hungry.

Bruce and Unitus were talking about strategies in warfare with several of the Federal agents.

Trevor said, "Let's take it in my den after we eat. Okay? The women get testy, if we are late for a meal!"

He raised his brandy glass and they raised their drinks, and they all said, "Here! Here!"

CHAPTER TWO

Corey was on the phone with Ellen and sexting. It was all they could do for a long time. "I want you so badly!'

"I can't believe we have been apart this long. For two years, I have seen you every day. It is awful what my body is saying," he was sitting in the bathroom talking to her.

"OH MY! Corey! I want you here with me, too," Ellen was not going to take a picture except of her breast. "They miss you!" she licked her finger slowly.

Corey said, "I am breaking out of jail tonight!"

"You cannot. I forbid you to get yourself killed over me," Ellen yelled into the phone.

"You are killing me right now. You will be eighteen in three days. You and I are getting married! No one can stop us and I can have you any time I want, and anywhere I want to as long as you say I can. Isn't that right, sweetheart?" Corey stated it as a fact.

"Anyway you want me," Ellen moaned.

"I may never come out of this bathroom," he sucked in a deep breath and finished what he was doing. He took a few minutes.

"That's when she lost it! I can't believe you did that without me. I will ….." she did and it was driving him mad.

"O O O! Now I feel better. How do you feel?" she asked.

"With one hand!" He laughed. "I love you! I got to go eat FOOD! I'll call you later." he sadly hung up.

Corey saw his mother sitting with Marcus and he was relieved. He had washed, but he was so in love with that girl. He needed to get some advice from Tate.

He wandered over to where Tate and Debbie were sitting after he fixed his plate.

"Where's your shadow?" Tate asked.

"She's not here," Corey frowned.

"I meant Jason," Tate said eyeing Corey closely. "Man your face is red and you're all sweaty." He laughed. "If I didn't know better, I'd say you had been...." Tate almost said what he was thinking.

"I told you, she is not here!" Corey's face softened. "You've been through it. You know how bad it is. What am I going to do? We want to get married SOON!"

"Have you told Aunt Eunice?" Tate asked.

"Oh God No, and don't you dare!" Corey bristled.

"Man eat your food before someone comes to check on you," Tate looked at Debbie.

"Honey, why don't you give Ellen a call? Tate needs a man to man talk to, and she may need a woman to talk to."

"Good Idea! She has just about drove me nuts tonight and tell her that!" Corey looked at Debbie.

"If you tell her to sit on ice cubes, she might do it," Corey smiled at the thought of that. Then he thought of how hot she was! He was going to embarrass himself. He sat closer to the table. He was thinking of putting ice down his pants, and he started shaking his head as if to get that out of his mind.

"Are you okay, son?" Eunice asked.

Corey quickly answered, "It was a fly buzzing around my head. I'm fine. Are you and Mr. Marcus doing okay?"

He could see how people could not believe his mother was single after seven years. His father, he remembered would pick her up, and swing her around like one of the kids. Until now, he had not known the meaning of true love, and all he wanted to do was swing Ellen around.

Eunice walked off, "Okay get that fly," Corey was shaking his head again. The thought of swinging Ellen from the rafter and her falling down on him, was unnerving him.

"Tate help us ... get married. Tell me what to do? I have a little money saved up from my job with Roscoe and my bike is paid off. I have to convince Mom to let us live with her for a little while. If we go on and get married, she can only let us stay. Right?" Corey was begging for help.

"I've been there. We will help AFTER this is over. You can't leave and she can't come here. These people will kill her, and you with no second thought. Tell her that. Debbie and I were about to go crazy before we got married. The wait was worth it! Man, I do know how bad it is!" Tate declared.

"Debbie, I am so glad you called," Ellen said.

"Corey is about crazy just like Tate was before we got together," Debbie admitted.

"Oh we are together ... but we are so ready to get married," Ellen admitted. "OOPS! I should not have said that. "I love him so much and miss him terribly."

Jana and Adriana were talking recipes. Adriana had finally got that delicious chicken recipe that Unitus was suppose to have cooked for her.

Jana said, "This man … they are talking about is so evil. He would line us all up and laugh while he shot us … one by one!" she shivered.

Adriana was not frightened. She had dealt with the mafia in court. The same was said to her about those horrible men.

"As long as the justice system works, I will put them away!"

"No matter how badass they think they are," Adriana was not saying that if they were trying to hurt Unitus or Angel, she would kill them with her own bare hands.

Jana said, "I worked for the CIA and thought I was all that, but my boss was Jung's biggest contact in the USA. He moved more heroin and cocaine than the Mexican cartel.

Does that not baffle the mind. Bruce and Unitus stopped his operation, and that is why he hates the Smiths. Poor Kyleigh was my boss's victim! That girl was put through hell. You must not say anything in front of her or she may relapse."

Jana paused again, "We together shut JUNG down. For awhile anyways, and it hurt his bank account. So Unitus is as anxious as Bruce, to get this kingpin."

She was staring at Adriana, "WE have to sit on those two and I mean SIT. This is why my husband cut Jared Banks. He says he didn't want to kill him. Just wanted to cut him as he had cut Kyleigh and brutalized her." Adriana's face had paled and she understood now better than before.

"Why didn't Bruce tell me this during the trial?" Adriana asked Jana.

"He said it was no use. You would have not believed him.

Unitus was his main concern, to get him out of that prison.

You do realize because they were CIA that they could not say ANYTHING! Unitus went to prison undercover to protect my Bruce. It is something I can talk to you about now because we have time, and a lot of time to talk!" Jana was squirming in her chair unable to sit still.

"I need you to understand that I did not know Bruce was in Japan undercover working on bringing Jung down. I fell in love with my husband and married him right away before I got my degree. My multilingual skills is what the CIA wanted me for. My degree in criminal justice made it better. Bruce supported me in anything I wanted to do."

She paused and looked around to make sure no one was listening. "Then I was made to believe my wonderful husband was a criminal, and I was devastated to see him in prison. There in that heinous place our love prevailed, and he told me the truth ... because I would not … could not give up on our love. That is why I need your help in keeping Bruce and your Unitus here with us! They will go to battle and we may never see either of them again, if we don't band together."

Adriana hugged Jana, and the men folks walked in.

Unitus said, "I want some of that!"

Bruce said, "Me, too!"

They all hugged and talked about the baby which was being held nonstop. Adriana looked at Unitus, "Yes, dear. We are going to have to expand her lungs again, when get home."

Marcus was not going to stay put. So Trevor and he, plus his entourage went to the construction company to see how much had been done on the THE HOTEL & THE CASINO. The groundwork had been completed and the architect Bryant Adams, also reviewed the layout of Marcus's home.

"This is the time to let me know, if you want to make any changes. I have the crews working around the clock. Let's look at the models of all three. I can change the marble color to this one and make the mosaic stonework more appealing. The fountains, I have moved to four locations that will make the entrance more grand. If you agree, I'll get you to initial each page."

He inked them and told Bryant, "Use your creative judge-ment. I trust you because you have never let me down on any of my other projects."

"Thank you sir. I will do my best!" and he and Marcus shook hands. Bryant turned and shook Trevor's, "It was nice meeting you. I hope to see you again in the near future."

"I'm going to get him to do my dock and boathouse. Soon as this mess is done. We can take the boat out, and fish on the lake, or we can fish off the dock!" Trevor said out loud his dream that was going to be built in the future .

"Sounds good to me. By then it'll be midwinter, but I kind of like it here, more and more every day. Sitting on the dock watching the snow melt looking at the mountains while the sun sets." They both chuckled.

"We have to get back before we get in REAL trouble."

Beatrice was telling Kyleigh how cute Madison looked in his jeans, and she was telling her how precious the girls looked in their pink frilly dresses.

"Kyleigh! Let's go shopping? Those skinny jeans really worked on Roscoe, too. Got to get some more, if I want a set of triplets … ten years from now … I just want sex, now!"

"Me, too!" Kyleigh ran for the computer.

They sat for two hours looking and ordering, but mostly for the kids. Then back to the lingerie and naughty stuff. Giggling all the while, until they got caught!

Guy and Roscoe came around the corner, "So this is where you two have been plotting. Let me see if I like what my wife ordered. Oh my! Yes I do indeed, and when might this care package be delivered?"

Trevor came in and said, "No packages can be delivered. Do put that on hold, PLEASE! I want nothing to come in from anyone that has not been thoroughly inspected by that team of experts. OK?"

Roscoe said, "Clearly we didn't think about that. So glad you pointed that out to the girls. You both know better than enticing us men at our on grandma's house," he made them all laugh.

"OH my goodness Trevor I ordered," Madeline whispered it in his ear.

"There maybe one exception!" Trevor said.

Roscoe and Guy said, "NO WAY, do you get to have fun and not us! This is a two way street!" pointing to himself then to them.

"A chocolate cake for my birthday! I'll let the dog sniff it!" Trevor whined then frowned.

"The boys are right, Madeline! No Cake … No packages of any kind." He rubbed his stomach and repeated, "Chocolate cake … never thought I'd turn down chocolate cake."

MAdeline started rubbing his stomach, "He just wants to watch his figure, boys. That's the only reason except he LOVES us more than cake!"

GM kissed him on the cheek.

Trevor pulled her ponytail.

CHAPTER THREE

Guy told Trevor he had to take Kyleigh to her doctor's appointment. They took five men and three vehicles. She was anxious and clung to Guy.

"It's okay honey! I am here with you," he kissed her neck.

It is something about this white limo that makes me want to strip your clothes off!'

"Why don't you and forget about the doctor?" she stared at him like she did on their honeymoon in the white limo.

"I'd love to, but we are here, and you wanted to come yesterday. You can have as much time as you need, and I will be here in the waiting room," Guy said as they walked into the doctor's office.

The session lasted an hour, and she had been crying because she had a tissue in her hand. Kyleigh gave Guy her printout. Her scripts had been faxed to the drugstore.

"We will cause a scene, if we go in there. They can't send them by package or Trevor will flip."

He called the pharmacist and had him bring them to the car and give them to James. The windows were tinted so no one could see inside the limo.

They sped off to go back to Southfork. The long ride gave them a chance to talk, but neither wanted to talk. "Avoiding the subject will not make it go away Guy," she said.

"Madeline told you," he said. She said,"You should have."

Lonestar, Haruto, and Minato met at Trevor's to look on his magic screen where the last reported whereabouts of Jung and his men were. The radar was indicating Boston harbor, Miami, and Galveston. The ports were being monitored.

Lonestar took Boston, Haruto took Miami, and Minato took Galveston. Each would mingle with the dock locals, and get info on his next shipment, or if Jung was looking for an expert to hire. They would volunteer for the job.

The first person Lonestar saw on the dock was Jeff Sanders. He did not see Lonestar. He thought Jeff would stay in Vietnam. If he is on the street, then he had accepted the contract for hire. Jung would fed his drug habit. Lonestar would keep him in view and pinpoint his trail for all to see.

He reported to Trevor and he was angry. Jeff had let Trevor down and now he was dealing with Jung to assassinate his family.

"Semper fi," Lonestar would contact Haruto and Minato.

Each had found a contract for hire man that they would follow.

"Seems he has them coming from everywhere. So this town will be crawling with hit men before the week is out!" Trevor was talking to the Federal agents and Marcus.

"Trevor you said it was bad. I just had no idea how bad. My men are at your disposal."

"We must protect our loving families," he looked worried for the first time since the restaurant explosion.

Roscoe, Guy, Unitus, and Bruce were listening closely.

Beatrice ran up the stairs chasing Cain and Caleb. There was a movie theater upstairs, and they wanted to see "Mickey Mouse." Madison was right behind them, and Kyleigh followed Beatrice into the room.

"If they will sit, the climb was worth it. The nanny has BeBe and FiFi, so let's recline."

The kids sat still as mice and watched the cartoons. Beatrice and Kyleigh were chatting away. Kyleigh told Beatrice about her appointment. "It helped me get some anger out!"

Beatrice said, "That is good. Don't keep it inside!'

Adriana and Angel came in, "So this is the new hideaway. Very nice ... PRIVATE screening. I must not tell Unitus, he would live in here. He likes to watch old cowboy movies. Yuck!"

Beatrice said, "I bet you like the murder mysteries or detective mysteries?"

Adriana replied, "Can't pass up a good romance or a whodunit! Guilty as charged!" and laughed.

Tate, Jason, and Corey were playing on the Wi Fi bowling and boxing games.

Madeline, Debbie, Jana, and Eunice were gathered around the kitchen island as the housekeeper shared some of her favorite quick fix recipes. She had cooked for some rich clients in her prime. She had carved roses of the radishes and the carrots she had julienne and placed in an ice cube bath. Then she twisted them around a toothpick and it became a curly pig's tail. "Just garnishes for the plates that add flair."

The dogs were playing all together and were so excited to see the trainer bring TNT, the last of the puppies to be trained. “Where is this special lady named Adriana that had borrowed Blackie from Mr. Trevor?”

Adriana came to see her new dog, “Boy do I like his name,” rubbing his head and sitting on the ground to play.

“I really need to train him in your house so when you’ all go up the mountain for good, give me a call,” then the trainer got in her van and was gone.

Adriana took her cell phone out and call Unitus and told him, and he came out to see the beautiful Black Russian Terrier.

“Guess what his name is?” Adriana had a twinkle in her eyes.

His brow furrowed, “Haven’t a clue! Maybe Stallion?”

“No, honey! That’s your name!” Adriana said. He grinned.

“Okay I give. What’s his name?” Unitus crossed his arms and waited.

They all shouted, “TNT.”

“Isn’t that a perfect name for our dog?” Adriana smiled.

“Yep, we are loud parents,” he almost said explosive.

That would not have been appropriate in their situation.

“How did that mother dog have all male puppies, but one,” Adriana asked. Trevor said, “I ordered it that way so we would not have one hundred and one!”

They all raised their fists and said, “Here! Here!”

A month went by and Machi and Mutsumi had not heard from their husbands and they were so worried. Machi called Trevor to ask, if he had heard from them. No one had, but he reassured the women soon as he heard, he would phone them. If they needed anything, he told them to let him or Bruce know.

They were working on their Japanese dolls and put them in individual glass display cases. The two were meticulous about their doll's Japanese clothing. Each detail had to be an exact replica of a real geisha's attire.

The tiny painting on the dolls faces had to be exactly as if the geisha, herself had applied it. These projects kept their minds occupied. They sold them for $150 each and always had a buyer on their website. Plus one store in New York bought them and sold them for double their asking price.

They could continue to stay at the motel and pay their own way. Machi was so worried though. She knew her husband was in harm's way, and she could not bring herself to tell her sister, how dangerous this mission was for their menfolk.

She did not worry when the two men were together. The men were unstoppable, but separate was different. They didn't have each other to cover their backs.

Machi convinced Mitsumi to stay with her at night, and they would work out of Mitsumi room during the daytime. So this would be their routine until their husbands came home.

They knelt and prayed together at night for their husbands safe return.

Roscoe and Guy went by the Smith Security Service building with several agents. They wanted to checked on things. Also swung by the GM & GS Private Investigation Service building from where the SBI were operating. The fax began ticker-taping a report from Haruto. "I have a lead and am in pursuit . They are moving in ... Beware … Fedex trucks … packages, Bruce."

Minato also ticker-taped a report . "Made contact … Beware Amtrak … luggage, Bruce."

Lonestar would not chance any mode of cyber-technology. He phoned Trevor with a disposal phone. "I have my eye on the prize! Trevor," nothing more. That prize was Jeff.

Trevor said, "This waiting is getting on my nerves."

Marcus said, "Mine too! Our men are doing a great job!"

Trevor said while pacing in the den, "In the next twenty-four hours... all hell is going to break loose. Bruce, Roscoe and Guy need to know now. I'm going to phone them."

The women and children were doing their usual daily routine. Only Corey was on the phone day and night with Ellen. He told Tate they had to go into town. "You got to help me or I am going alone. We are going to get married today!"

They went and found the Justice of Peace to marry them. Corey and Ellen had been planning this by phone for a month. It went smoothly so she went back with them.

Eunice was furious. She looked from Tate to Corey.

"We are both eighteen. It was my decision!" Corey put his arms around Ellen.

"I am angry that you left here! You do not understand that someone is trying to kill us. You and Ellen may not know better, but Tate you do!" Eunice was mad that her nephew had helped in this fiasco.

She turned and went to her room.

Corey told Jason, "You gotta find another room and find it now. Go see Mom," and he shut the door.

CHAPTER FOUR

Ellen was in his arms as he locked the door.

He had her on the bed and entered her before she could take a breath. "Corey... the others? Oh my whatever. Just don't stop!" she was gasping.

"You can make love to me. I just had to have us joined for it is the most awesome feeling. Do you feel it?" he was stroking her hair and holding on till she said she could.

He was pulsating and she was rearing to get his full length just right and it was just incredible. The sensations were causing her to squeeze and release, driving him to grab her buttocks tighter and tighter till it erupted into shock waves. Electrifying them both until they could not breath.

"Corey help me ... That's it!" she trembled. It was him that was needing her. "We are ... I feel it. Kiss me ... quick ....or I will yell my love for you."

She kissed him and he yelled into her mouth as he reached the pinnacle. She had just before him and clung to him pulling his buttocks tighter to her.

"We are one and no one can pull us a part from this day forward," Corey was kissing Ellen all over. They never came out of their room that night.

They put a sign on their door, "JUST MARRIED."

She did not want to face his mother. "I cannot go out there."

"Yes you can. I am here for you now. Smile!" he said.

"You can bring me food. I will go out tomorrow. Just let me be with you, and only you alone today."

"Did you take your pill?'" Corey did not want anyone to say that they HAD to get married. Neither did she.

"I did yesterday, but I need to get my pocketbook and take today's." He brought her pocketbook, "We will plan our family after all this dies down." He gave her a glass of water and then started kissing her navel and her legs. She was writhing and he came up to her breast, "I have missed these," he kissed on one and then the other.

"Corey honey you got me right where you want me and you had better do something before I explode without you."

They went together over and over, melding their limbs together, in a give and take motion.

They didn't stop till the wee hours of the morning.

"I want you to be real satisfied and never look elsewhere," Corey said.

"You are all I have ever wanted," Ellen lay her head on his bare chest.

It was their first realization, "WE are so so MARRIED and I am so so glad we did this. One more day and I would have done something so so stupid," Corey said.

"Like what?" Ellen asked.

"Like walk out of here all by myself," and he meant it.

He said, "You are mine now."

"You will never go a day without this," and he kissed her lips. **FINALLY … YES!** they slept.

Jason was playing games and Eunice told him he could sleep in her room. "There are twin beds in my room. Corey should have told you and I, but it is okay as long as everyone is safe," Eunice hugged her baby boy.

"You are right Mom. Will Ellen come and live with us?" Jason asked genuinely concerned.

"I guess we will have to ask Corey," she said. "Corey has nowhere else to go." He had the part-time job and now he has graduated. He and she could both get a job and move on.

Eunice did not want to face this tonight. Jason went and played more games and Marcus came and sat beside her.

"How are you doing, Dear?" he asked Eunice. He could see she was devastated. She may need to talk to someone. He patted her hand that was lying on the sofa. He saw Jason and would talk to him, later.

"I'm in shock, but I am adjusting because there is nothing I can do. They are both eighteen," Eunice looked at Marcus. "I so wanted him to go to college, but he has a mind of his own. I use to say that skateboarding was going to be his life. Now?" she shrugged her shoulders.

"He is in love and he has thought about this for awhile. I've seen him about to climb the walls while talking to someone on his cell phone. I assumed it was a girl and voila. Here she is! He will not want to leave here anymore as long as she is here. How long have they been dating?"

"Almost two years. She helped him bring his grades up from D's to A's. She is a smart girl. He would have married her anyway after all this. At least, I don't have to worry about where he is now," Eunice laughed to keep from crying.

Marcus nodded. "Young love is grand. Almost as grand, as my friendship with you, is growing. How do feel about me? Do you think I stand a chance with you?"

She gasped, "Jason is in this room another change for him would not be good."

"He can't hear us. He has the headset on." He took both her hands in his, and repeated, "Do I stand a chance with you?"

"Yes I ...I think you do. Only if you go slow. I do not want to be pressured. I need time to adjust. Even the thought makes my head spin."

"Good," and Marcus kissed her hand and walked to Jason to see how he was doing.

Marcus played a card game with Jason and looked into Eunice's eyes as he played.

"Would it be okay, if we asked your mother to play?" Marcus asked Jason.

"She don't know how!" he looked at his Mom sitting by herself. "But if you want, we can teach her how. Be patient Mr. Marcus, she is a slow learner," Jason smiled.

Marcus laughed, "I will if you will," and they shook hands. Jason asked his Mom to come and play and she did.

They played for hours. Marcus had never took the time to play games with Adriana when she was Jason's age. He did have regrets because this was really a fun night.

Adriana saw her father playing cards with them, and motioned for Unitus to come to see. "Isn't that the sweetest? Eunice is making a different man outta my daddy."

"Yeah the right woman will make a man do just about anything," Unitus cupped her rear and she swatted at him.

"Oh! It's on tonight!" Adriana grinned at him and he knew what she was thinking.

"I think tonight is right now. Angel is asleep, so I am lusting after my wife. Can you help my pain?" Unitus was not going to take no for an answer.

He picked her up and threw her across his shoulder and marched to their room.

"Caveman! I have a bone to pick with you!" she was scratching his back with her nails were driving him wild when she stretched her legs. Finally they were inside their room. No denial that she couldn't wait ... only tearing his shirt off … meant he would do the same. Skin against skin was the beginning of their lustful night.

He could only moan, as she wiggle herself and he laid her down slowly not to disengage their coupling, and she begged for him to go, and he would not. He wanted it to last for her to climax before him. Then he would bring her up again and again till they both could not take anymore. Collapsing in the flow of the moment, "You are the best!" Adriana said.

"No you have the best… I need you always to give me your all and I will take all that you give. You are amazing!"

"We are amazing! Unitus not many married couples have what we have," she spoke softly into his ear.

They showered and went and got the baby and played with Angel until she was tired again, and Unitus winked.

Adriana licked her lips. He knew when they got started the night was still young and their passion had just had an appetizer. He was going to give her the full entree, when the baby went back to sleep again. Adriana was squeezing her legs together, so he could see her need. "Stop it or else our baby is going to witness how much her daddy loves her mommy."

Angel went to sleep and they slowly savored each others' body again and again until the wee hours of the morning. "Adriana are you trying for baby number two?" Unitus asked.

She licked her smiling lips and reached for him.

Tate and Corey were talking the next morning. Tate said, "Your mother is angry with me and I can't blame her. We can not go away from here again. The WIVES are our responsibility now," pointing to himself then to Corey.

"Yes she is, because Trevor has scared her to death. He says there are hit men from three different places coming here," Corey said. "Where did you hear that?' Tate frowned.

"I was eavesdropping on him and Roscoe with the Feds," Corey admitted.

"If Trevor says it, then it is so! We have to make plans of what we can do to keep the women and children safe,"

Tate was antsy and started pacing.

"I got to talk to Roscoe tomorrow. He has turned in for the night, but I'll ambush him in the morning. Thanks for telling me," Tate said.

"We are all in it together. Let me know what he says," and Corey went to the kitchen for a soda. He swung by to say goodnight to Jason who was enjoying Marcus and his Mom's company. So he went straight to his honeymoon suite.

His bride was showering. Hmm ...looks good to me, and in he went with her.

"No one should be as happy as I am with you Ellen," Corey said.

"Only married people feel like this because they have the love of their life from sunup to sundown," Ellen said as she started kissing him on his back.

Turning to face her, he said, "I am a happy married man!"

Bruce and Jana had rode the horses around Southfork today and he told her, "We can't do it anymore. The word is from Haruto and Minato that two hit men are on their way. Trevor is livid that Lonestar told him that Jeff Saunders is the third man for hire. It is insane to think as close as he was to Trevor in the military that he would do something to harm us now."

Jana replied, "He is a man that is overtaken by his disease. Addiction will make a person do things that they would not ever think that they would do. So sad, but I am glad Lonestar has an eye on him, and not you. You have to keep both your eyes on me! Do you hear me? Me Bruce ... on me," and she was getting off the horse in the barn when he grabbed her up to his saddle.

"I have my eyes and hands on you my love, and you were looking so good bouncing on that horse that I caught myself wishing it was me, you were riding," and she settled against him in the saddle. She was so small that they fit so well in the man sized saddle, but if one moved it would make the other shiver and strain.

She turned around and put her arms around his neck, "and where might you want to ride to?" He was staring into her eyes, "to cherry blossom land."

Their honeymoon was so special in the cherry blossoms of Japan. They had made love every other hour, and she knew he was saying he wanted her all through the night.

"We will scare this horse too death and then have to explain what happened. Let me take you inside or not?" she had unbuttoned his jeans and her little hands were performing magic. There was no way he was going to get her into the house, and she smiled her sweet smile. They slid down the horse and went into the tack room.

She was straddled around his waist as he walked there, her bottom was bumping on him that made him tighten.

"You got to stop or I will be through before you get started," Bruce was taking her Jodhpurs off in one swift motion and her lacy panties with them. She lie there looking at him, he was tugging at his jeans. She said, "Let me."

"I want to savor you. You are as passionate now, as you were the day I wed you," and they made love.

CHAPTER FIVE

Trevor was standing on the porch when he heard a shot fired. The men were hustling to get the women and children into the basement.

The two sets of twins were loving their mom and dad who put them under their arms and went running. They giggled.

But not Madison, his mother was crying and his daddy was holding her instead of him. He climbed onto his father's back. Then he was happy.

Tate and Debbie were gathering the honeymoon couple.

Madeline grabbed her derringer and told the nanny to take Angel, and for them and the housekeeper to get below.

Marcus had Eunice and Jason went downstairs in a flash.

GM knew she would not until Trevor came in. Adriana would not till Unitus came in. Jana would not till Bruce came in. The men were stubborn, but the women were stubborner.

Madeline asked Trevor, "You have men, you have Feds, you have Marcus's men. Why are you and the boys standing out here like fools?"

"Oh my lord, GM didn't say that!" Roscoe said to himself.

"All is well. It was probably just a hunter," Trevor said.

Then he saw Lonestar, and he was dragging a wounded Jeff with him.

He told Trevor, "He is now yours. I figured you could get more information out of him when he was alive. Believe me, I wanted him dead. No way would he live, if he had harmed anyone of you . The Feds had better get him and lock him up, before I change my mind."

Trevor hugged Lonestar, his true friend and thanked him, after the Feds had Jeff and carted him off.

"There are no words to express our gratitude."

Lonestar asked, "Have you heard from the Japanese brothers?"

"Not a word," Trevor said.

"I am not as confident in how they work, and fear they maybe in trouble. I will check and see, if I can find them." Lonestar left through the woods.

Bruce was worried, too. He did not want Jana to see how worried. He turned to talk to Roscoe and Guy.

"We cannot go help Lonestar," Unitus told Bruce. "Don't even think it!"

"You are one to talk," Bruce stared at Unitus.

He had his blade leg on … meant for running. Adriana had not seen him change to warrior mode and that was a good thing. He was not going to let anyone harm his new found family. So Bruce might as well step away.

Bruce said, "Do I have to tackle you right here. There is enough man power. We have to stay back encase the women and children need us. Yes, Adriana and Angel! Think man!"

"Yes you and I, both put ourselves out there often, but we had no one! Now … we do! Our eyes must be on them, my friend! At all times!" Bruce's eyes never left Unitus's because he saw the killer instinct in them.

"You know me well. We have been through so much together and I know you are right, but the thought of someone hurting my Adriana or Angel, hits me in my gut!'

"They cannot make it in this world without you Unitus. That is the truth!" Bruce had to lay it on thick. His friend had almost gone out that door into the path of the crazies.

"You are right for a change, Bruce!" Unitus laughed and hugged him as the women came out of the basement.

Trevor wanted to talk to that "sorry piece of crap" called Jeff, but he knew the Feds would be interrogating him thoroughly and he didn't want to interfere. Jeff would be in withdrawals in the next twenty four hours. They would have to confine him, but good. Or else, Jeff was clever enough to escape. He talked to the head of the team and voiced his concerns.

Madeline was on his arm and she saw it in his eyes. "Yes, you are my hero. You only have to keep yourself safe for me because I can't make it a day without you, Trev!"

"I will keep you and the rest safe. So you stop worrying," kissing her ponytail.

They turned and walked in together. Everyone was on edge.

"He is behind bars, so everyone get back to the normal things that you do. I'm hungry who's cooking me or you, Madeline?"

"He's back to normal. He is hungry. Yes Trevor. I am cooking!" she said.

They all laughed and returned to helping prepare meals, and change baby diapers, and the honeymooning continued.

Haruto was beaten and robbed by the men that hired him.

"You are not going to have any money or think you are better than us on this job, boy," Haruto held himself in check not to display his fighting abilities, too soon.

They had to prove themselves superior to him or they would slit his throat with no second thought. He nodded to them that he would obey them.

The bruises healed and he pulled his load on Jung's smuggling route in Miami. The word was he had a hit man by the name of "Raven." He thought that was a weird name for a man and he ask about this "Raven" amongst the workers and they laughed.

"It is not a he … It is a she. She is an evil woman ... the deadliest black widow! That is … Raven. She is beautiful and just as deadly as the spider. You are warned," the little Japanese man bowed.

No one bowed unless out of respect or trickery. This man was trying to trick him. So he would thank him for the info, but he would watch him closely.

The days were long and finally the Raven came to visit the boss. Jung was so into his heroin that he grabbed the Raven. She whipped out her switchblade and had it at his throat.

She spat in his face. "Do you want me to work for you or not? If you do ... you had better never lay a hand on me again or I will kill you. Do you hear me JUNG?" she hissed.

He laughed, "Not if I kill you first!" and they both laughed, but he didn't put his hands on her again.

The mission was set to go to North Carolina. Raven was leading. She had frowned at Haruto and he looked at the ground. He must not stare or have any eye contact with her. Otherwise, she would not choose him to go.

She walked up to him and rubbed her leg against him and he gasped as if scared, and that pleased her. "Him and him will go. No one else." She was staring at him to see his reaction. He gave no reaction. Just stone faced and said, "As you wish," and bowed.

She was intrigued, she was going to break him down. He knew it, and she knew it! Haruto was a fine looking Japanese man, and the Raven was a woman of insatiable desire. She knew she could get any man that she wanted, but this man was different. Hmm ... he had not lusted after her as the others had.

She would find out why? If it killed him ... she laughed.

They were packed and on their way by van. If they took a plane, her name would be a tip off.

She was wearing black leather pants that fit like a second skin, and pointed toe black boots with three inch heels. The pants left nothing to the imagination, and her tiny breast needed no bra. When she was talking to Haruto, her tits were protruding through her thin black shirt. He knew it and she knew it, because she gulped as his eyes looked straight at them instead of her face.

This pleased her that he was indeed a man of passion. She would have him before the trip was over and it wet her leather crotch which made her mad. He was having the power.

"Damn it!" she said to herself.

She went to the restroom, and he went to the men's room. She came in with him and locked the door. He kept on peeing as if she were not there. She came up behind him, "I just was curious ... what you had under there."

She was fondling him, and he without being able to control it was hardening, and she was loving it. He was trying so hard not to react. He had to satisfy her or he was a dead man, but it was more than that. He was enjoying it so much that he climaxed first, then she laughed. He then gave it to her, and she was lost and screaming with the fulfillment. He had wanted her to get it all and be happy. She wanted more and told him. "I need that again. Can you or can't you?"

He frowned and he held on to her shoulders, and he drove it in like a jackhammer until she was sated. He closed his eyes. He was so satisfied. He was so ashamed.

"Don't look so frightened! I will keep you as my play toy! I will not kill you unless you cannot satisfy me. You did good!

You did damn good! O my, I want you again."

Haruto was not going to die from a gunshot or knife wound. He was going to die, if he could not perform. This is the worst, best assignment ... he had ever had. This woman was messing with his mind. He was dying just thinking of their tryst. OH NO Machi would never understand. Now he was only thinking of Raven, and she had his soul in her hand, and he wanted her again.

He told her, "Raven I need you please!" and she let him in the back of the van. He made it worth her while. She was screaming his name as the driver had Bose headphones on listening to music. They were trying to kill each other to see who wanted it more, and who was the strongest. Haruto had by now lost all his sexual inhibitions and was dominating her, and she was loving it.

"Where have you been all my life? You are my equal Haruto! You are stronger than you look. No one has ever thrown me down and took what they wanted, but you. You know I will have to kill you or you will have to kill me, but until then hold me and make love to me. Tomorrow will take care of itself!"

Haruto said to himself, "She is going to make me lose my mind, so don't think about what she is doing right now." She was holding him and doing what she said she would never do, and he was coming undone anew. She had him begging.

"Please you are killing me!" She had him wanting to die to have her. She climbed on him, and reared back grabbing her ankles, and rode him to the stars.

He knew he was a dead man. He was her slave now.

Minato was not as lucky. He was with a lot of badass Japanese that thought they were Texans. It was Galveston with a twist. The shipment had come in and Jung had put the word out that he was looking for a hit man, and Minato met and took the job. The ones with him were just locals with no talent except to report back, nothing of substance in between.

They also drove to North Carolina, but on a semi-truck and their transportation was not comfortable, just cramped and smelly.

Minato was longing to be with his bride. This was not the assignment he wanted, but one that had to be done.

It would take a couple of days. So he was going to get some much needed sleep.

Unlike his brother who was awake all day and all night.

They had not been in contact since they left, and Minato was thinking about giving him a call, but brother had said no calls unless someone is shot.

Lonestar had located Minato. He was following the semi since they left the truck stop. He knew these men would spill their guts about Jung, if the Feds got them alive.

So he was going to report to Trevor and see what could be arranged. They told him to follow and keep them posted that a roadblock would be set up. All the agents were aware of what Minato looked like and not to fire at him for any reason.

Lonestar had not found Haruto.

That was not a good sign.

Haruto was trying to talk Raven into abandoning this mission. "You are what I have wanted all my life."

"But Haruto this is my job. I have to do it! Or I am a dead woman. You know that. Why are you talking like this?"

"I want you and I cannot have you, if you are dead. It is your choice to walk away with me now or we both get killed. It would take a strong woman to walk away. I think you are strong and love me enough to do it!" Haruto stared at her.

"Who said I loved you?" she scowled and hissed.

He grabbed her and kissed her so deep that she moaned.

"So I am in love with the sex. What we have is that love? It is a feeling that I have NEVER had before. Wanting someone else all the time is new. I agree it is wonderful, but it cannot last. Can it?" She was puzzled... in her world sex had meant pain ... not love. It meant weakness … not strength. Confused she was. He was messing with her mind.

"It will only get better and better. I promise I have held back until I know you are mine forever, and that is what love is. I will give you my all, if you will give me your all. I did not meanfor this to happen. I did not want this to happen, but I am into you, as deep as you will let me be. Now think about us as a normal couple. If we could take down Jung together, they would give us both immunity, and we could have each other all day and night for the rest of our life. FREE!"

"What the f ... are you saying? Take Jung down are you crazy?" Raven was not hearing him right.

"Yes crazy over you!" Haruto grabbed her and showed her.

He told her, "Just stay behind me and I will protect you!Raven do you hear me?" She had a job to do and he would not protect her because he was in love with her meant nothing OR did it. She was torn. They were at the house and he got out and held his hands in the air. The driver shot him and she shot the driver, and ran to Haruto. Raven ran and ran for Haruto, and knelt by him.

Trevor had the Feds take him to the hospital and Raven into custody.

Haruto said, "Trevor, she will help you to get Jung. Just tell her I am ALIVE, whether I am or not. Tell her I want her to help you, and she will as long, as she thinks I am alive!"

Bruce was there to go with Haruto to the hospital, "Bruce promise me not to tell my wife unless I die. I DO NOT want her at the hospital. I want Raven there, please understand!"

"I do my friend. Now don't talk," and Bruce held his hand.

When they got to the hospital they worked on him, and he did not respond. After the second shock he came around, he had to be stabilized before they could do surgery to get the bullet out.

Raven was beside herself, "Yes whatever Haruto wants me to do, I will do it. Tell him that!" She asked the Federal agent,

"He said that if I helped I could get immunity, is this true?"

"If you help and we get Jung, you will be FREE as a bird," the agent said in front of Trevor.

"He believes in a Mr. Trevor, so I will do it! Jung will never expect me to betray him, and I would not, if not for Haruto!"

Lonestar wanted to tell Machi, but Trevor said not. There was a reason. The roadblock was set and the semi fell into the trap, and Minato was rescued. Jung's men were in custody and the Feds would get the info they needed.

Raven was wired and took them to Jung. She walked in as usual and told him the job was done, and she wanted her money. When he went to get it, the Feds moved in and arrested him.

She was a smooth operator. She never cracked a smile just that bad to bone attitude had got her where she thought she wanted to go.

Jung swore, "I will get you Raven. I will get YOU … No matter where you go … I will get you!"

Raven did not flinch nor did she care what Jung said or did.

She turned to the agent and said, "Now can you take me to the hospital!"

JUNG would be in withdrawals for awhile and the Feds were going to build a case that his organization could not crack. They had him after all this time. This ONE WOMAN had taken him down.

She went into Haruto's hospital room. He had had surgery, and was on a ventilator and tubes everywhere. She just held his hand and talked to him ... and told him what she had done and that she LOVED him.

The alarm went off and he was gone. They could not revive him. He was gone.

The officer could not control her. She was crying and fighting staff... SCREAMING for them not to take him away.

They finally restrained her, and gave her a sedative.

She slept on the chair till the Feds could find her a safe house. She had no family and no contacts except the underworld, and they would kill her for certain.

She did not care at this point, if they did. It was all for naught anyways ... her first and ONLY love ... was gone as quickly as he came into her life.

He was gone out of her life forever.

She beat her fists on the sofa and cried, "WHY?"

"WHY did I trust you?"

She wailed because she knew why ...

"HE loved me!"

PART FIFTEEN

CHAPTER ONE

The relief that the kingpin had been captured was the best news to the Smith and Porter families. It made local, state, and national news.

Everyone was rejoicing and going back to their homes. Adriana and Unitus took little Angel back up the mountain to her beautiful nursery.

Guy took his smiling wife Kyleigh and son Madison, back to their home around the corner.

Roscoe and Beatrice took their set of twin boys, Cain and Caleb. Also they took their set of twin girls, BeBe and FiFi home with a mountain of supplies back to their house.

Eunice said to Jason and Corey, "It's about time for us to go home, too." Ellen was standing behind Corey. She added, "You too, Ellen. You are one of the family now. So let's get going. Marcus is going to give us a lift." They gathered their belongings and Jason jumped into the limo beside Marcus and said, "Geez this is a cool car, Mr. Marcus," and high-fived him. Eunice was smiling and the honeymooners were sitting close together lovey-dovey talking.

Tate and Debbie were getting their classes back in order.

Bruce and Jana were preparing to go and see Machi.

Haruto was Jana's cousin, so she would help her bury him with honors. How he talked that girl into helping capture Jung, was beyond her. It was because of HARUTO that the families were safe. Trevor had given her carte blanche, "anything they needed" would be paid for by them.

Minato was holding his wife, Mitsumi. Machi was numb and sat beside Jana and Bruce. The white limo went to the funeral home, and arrangements were made to transport him by plane to their hometown in Japan. He would be buried where Machi would be buried one day beside him.

Bruce and Jana would fly with the family and meet her parents at the airport.

Trevor and Madeline wanted to go to see the girl that had saved their lives. The Feds took them.

RAVEN was huddled in a ball on the bed. Madeline was shocked to see her all dressed in black. She sat beside her and introduced herself to her. Thanking her for everything that she had done.

"I didn't do it for you people … I did it for Haruto! He was my hero. He showed me what love is. I had never been loved. Now he is gone. I have nothing and nobody. They will find me. They will kill me and I can't even be buried beside him. This in itself may kill me. For what did I do this for! He said he had never known a love so intense as ours … and make no mistake... he was mine till the end of time. He said that to me!

He died because of me. He jumped in the way of the bullet to save me." She had to talk to someone and this lady was so kind … and her husband came and gave Raven a hug.

"You are not alone anymore. We are your family from this day forward. We cannot take you home yet. Once you get a new name and a new place and are SAFE. You can go back to school and we will take care of the expensive. We will visit and you can visit, when the two years is past. You can change your hair color, wardrobe, and come as an entirely different person to our home. You will always be WELCOME. Haruto wanted you to have a chance in life. If he was important to you, don't let it be for naught. Do something that you think he would want you to do. You are free of your past," said GM.

"That is what he said he wanted us to be ... is free. There is no us. I am not worth it," Raven said softly.

Trevor stepped forward, "Yes, you are my dear!" and he hugged her again. She cried and cried in his arms.

"Haruto said Mr Trevor was a good man… that he wanted to save your family. I see you two, are what he said. You are being good to me. I am just a hard case to crack. I will eventually make you proud of me. Two years from today! I will be at your door."

She was looking forward now. Their visit had made a difference. Raven was her real name, but what would it be in two years. The Federal agent said, "Soon as we get her settled and she is doing well, we will give you her name and address. It cannot be done now. Maybe six months is a good projection or a year. Trevor knows I will do the best for her."

"What happened to Jeff?" Trevor needed to know.

"He will not see the light of day for 100 years. Don't worry!"

Marcus went in with Eunice and Jason while Corey and Ellen hung back getting their luggage separated. Their room had to be decided upon by his mother, and she was occupied right now.

Marcus was not use to a small space with no amenities, but it was neat and a well maintained house. It had a comfortable sitting area, and she was fixing them some coffee.

Jason was showing him his model car collection that he had built. He had never known his dad so this fatherly experience was really making an impact on him.

Corey and Ellen came in and sat with them until Eunice brought the coffee in on a tray, and she asked if they would like a soda?

"Mom …we can get it. Just sit and enjoy your company. We will let you decide which room will be ours. There's no rush."

They walked to the kitchen. They were inseparable.

He was afraid Ellen would run home or something. He still could not believe, she had only talked to her mother once. "Do you want to call your mother?" Corey asked.

"No way. She would be over here in a New York minute. Your mother has enough to deal with without me adding to the list." Ellen was a levelheaded girl that knew what havoc her mother would bring with her. Corey kissed her cheek.

Jason asked Corey, if he could use his skateboard.

"Only if you look both ways and stay on the sidewalk. When you get sixteen I will give it to you, if you do well in school," Corey said. "Yay" said Jason and jumped in the air.

"Trevor that was the saddest grief-stricken young girl that I have seen in a long while. I think it was only right for us to ADOPT her. Thank you for being the man that you are. The most giving and thoughtful husband a woman could ask for … and you are mine. I love you dearly!" Madeline kissed him in their big house that was now almost vacant.

"You ... my darling are the love of my life. I know you will cherish a new charity case, and you will help mold her to be a southern belle. Mark my words! She has been brought into our lives FOR A REASON," Trevor said as an omen.

They got a call from Bruce and Jana that they had arrived safely in Japan, and that they would be home in a week.

Bruce was still cautious since his dealings with Jung had been on this side of the world, but he had to come and support Jana and her family in their lost.

Haruto had been a loyal friend and employee. Bruce wept at the graveside and said, "Till we meet again. Rest in peace."

Jana kissed his casket and Machi fainted. Minato and Mitsumi took her to the car. Nothing could ease her pain.

Jana's mother said she would be there for her as would her sister and Minato. Bruce turned to Minato and gave him a hug, "I am so sorry, if you need anything just give me a call. Do not worry! You are on my payroll forever, my friend."

Bruce told Jana they had done all that they could do, and that he thought that the faster they could leave was for the best. He saw too many familiar faces.

He was so thankful when they touched down at home safely.

The town was abuzz about the new hotel & casino. It meant many new jobs. No one seemed to realize that also there was a beautiful new mansion going up on the outskirts of town near the mountains around the bend from the Smith Lake.

Marcus was standing on the veranda talking to Trevor about how much longer it was going to take to complete his new home.

Trevor said, "Don't worry about how long Marcus... you are always welcome here. It isn't like we don't have the room," he chuckled. "Besides Madeline is a mother hen and she loves to fuss over her family and friends. Now that the family have all gone home, she is fussing and fussing over me," and Trevor grinned and winked at Marcus.

"Yeah, I've noticed you are really complaining a lot lately!" They both laughed.

"How is Eunice and the boys?" Trevor asked.

Now it was time for Marcus to blush, but he didn't. "Are you prying into my love life ... Trevor?" he gave him a mean scowl.

"You betcha, my friend!" He grinned and added, "GM and I got an investment in your relationship and we want to know if our dividends are paying off?" Trevor asked as he sipped his brandy and looked up at the mountain's horizon.

"I'd say it may double in value soon!" Marcus was looking at the same mountain, sipping his martini.

Trevor turned and looked at him without saying a word ... just a smile on his face.

"And?" Trevor nudged him.

"When the house is completed, I'm going to ask her to marry me. If she says yes, I will be a happily married man just like you!" Marcus continued to sip his martini.

Madeline came out and had not heard what was said, but both men were up to something. They did not grin both at the same time, unless something was up!

"Okay what did I miss? Don't you dare leave a single thing out. I need a good laugh, too!" Madeline sipped her ginger ale and flipped through her magazine until Marcus finished what he had just said. She was jumping from the lounger and running to give him a hug. "OH MY GOD, I am so happy for you my friend. I told Trevor just the other day," Trevor placed a hand on her shoulder and said, "Down mama, down!"

Marcus added, "Madeline, dear. I haven't asked her yet, and you cannot breathe a word to her. Do you promise?"

GM was sealing her mouth with an imagery key and she put the imagery key in her bra and patted it ... as if his secret was in her personal safe.

Trevor came and kissed his wife and said, "It had better stay a secret or I will break that safe open. I am a safe cracker Marcus in my spare time," and he rolled his eyes at his wife's breasts. They all laughed.

Marcus had asked Adriana to help him pick out the ring. She had chosen a Neil Lane diamond that she thought Eunice would like. She was so happy and made a promise not to let the cat out of the bag. She was so happy because it meant her father would be near and could watch her child grow up.

With Eunice there would be no pretense, and no gold digger status to upset her father's peace of mind. She just hoped her father would not get bored with Eunice.

Once they are engaged Adriana promised herself to take Eunice on some shopping trips. Adriana gasped and her lip curled up as if something stank, "I hate shopping! Maybe Unitus can take her!" she said to herself.

She threw her head back and cackled.

Unitus came running into the living room and asked, "What have I done now? You don't laugh like that unless I have screwed up. So?" lifting her high in the air.

"So tell me woman!" Unitus demanded.

"I am pregnant," she was almost dropped by a trembling man, and one that was devouring her mentally to say it again.

"You are saying, WE?" he was mumbling and his eyes were staring into hers.

"Yes! We are going to have a boy this time a little Unitus. I predict it!" he closed her mouth with the kiss that took her breath away.

Unitus was walking with her and Adriana was slipping onto his bulging area. The usual comfortable wrapping of her legs around his waist made it easier for him to walk.

To walk them to their bedroom because Angel was down for her nap, and they had things to celebrate in their own special incredible way.

"You are!" "No you are!" "Incredible!" "Yes, we are!"

CHAPTER TWO

There was a knock at the door and the dog went to see who was there. Madison was right behind the dog, and Kyleigh was right behind them both. She froze.

Her mother stood there. She had not called her daughter the hold time they were at Trevor and Madeline's.

"Hello Mother! Want you come in," she had Madison by the hand. He did not know who this woman was and stood behind Kyleigh hugging her legs.

"Madison come see your grandma!" Mrs Middleton said.

Guy came flying around the corner without looking, "GM, I was thinking ..." Then he stopped realizing it was not the real grandma. "Sorry! How are you ma'am?" and turned around and exited.

The woman was not his favorite person nor did he like her, but she was Kyleigh's mother.

"Where is father?" Kyleigh asked.

"Parking the car. He and I wanted to make sure you 'all were okay after this awful event." She was talking as if it was a social occasion that had gone bad.

"We are fine, mother. As you can see, Guy takes real good care of us!" and she smiled to see her mother assessing the house and all its grandeur.

That's all her mother had ever cared about was money and prestige. That was of least value to Kyleigh. She would live in a pup tent with Guy. He was her hero and a wonderful father.

She was thinking about everything to keep from having to talk to her mother until her father comes in.

Then she ran to him and kissed him. "I've missed you so much Daddy. How are you feeling?" she saw him limping.

He said, "Just a little arthritis. How's my girl and little Madison, where is his?"

"I'm fine and he's with Guy in the playroom. He loves the toy that you sent. He loves the action toys the most. I keep getting him educational stuff, but Guy says he needs to be a little boy and play first," and Kyleigh smiled.

"Let's go find them," and they went and left her mother sitting in her neat little spot as usual. She would not move from it.

"Mr. Middleton so good to see you, sir!" Guy shook his hand and gave him a hug. Guy truly enjoyed his company and Madison came running and jumped in his lap.

"Granddaddy," Madison then got down and ran and got the toy that granddaddy had got him.

"See daddy! He remembered," Kyleigh said and smiled.

"He is a fine son, Guy! Just like his father. How is your family? I know this has been traumatic for all of you. I have had you all in my prayers!" and he meant every word.

"Everyone is doing okay now, but it was scary there for awhile. Kyleigh has come through this like a trooper," and Guy hugged her. She nestled closer to him on the sofa.

"I guess I better go get mother. She will not move until I do."

He went and escorted her into the den where they were.

"Can I fix you a bite to eat?" Kyleigh asked.

"NO! We just ate," Mrs Middleton was quick to stop her daughter from showing off her cooking skills. She wanted all the accolades for cooking and no competition from her daughter.

Beatrice saw the Middleton's car at Kyleigh's and told Roscoe. "She is going to need me to talk to this evening so make plans with Guy."

They were glad to be at home, but they enjoyed their time together at GM's. Beatrice had all the support now with the nanny and the housekeeper, Kyleigh had no one, but GS.

Roscoe said, "I'm going on to work. I will call him when he gets to GM & GS Private Investigation Service. He says it is going to be his and grandma's again. Trevor doesn't know that GM is going back to work."

Beatrice said, "He is going to blow a gasket when he finds out! So don't you be the one to tell him," she kissed him at the door.

"Do I look crazy?" Roscoe asked.

"Don't answer that my love! You know I am crazy. Crazy in love with my red haired beauty with pale green eyes! I'm never going to get to work!" She smiled and kissed his neck.

"I repeat! I am never going to get to work. Go woman before I hurt myself getting to the Silverado. Holy! Moly!" he saw it in her eyes. She said, "I'll walk you out darling!"

"Would you?" Roscoe was chomping at the bit.

Roscoe knew Beatrice was going to get into that Silverado and beg him to join her on the back seat of that soft leather that they had enjoyed for years now. It made his day!

He went skipping up to the Smith Security Building and Inscoe met him. "Good morning, I see somebody got lucky last night!"

Roscoe straightened his tie at the front window before going in. He said, "You know me too well, Sgt. Inscoe. How's the wife and new boy at your house?"

"They are fine, but I haven't been lucky in awhile," and he emphasized by his flatfooted walk. His frown and nod was a riot. Roscoe chuckled and patted him on the back.

"All you need is two sets of twins and things will turn around for you, buddy!" Roscoe had to rub it in. Sarge only had the one newborn named Joe.

Inscoe was adjusting after a twenty year age difference in his children. This last one was a change of life baby. His miracle baby, he had said.

Roscoe's kids would grow up together with this kid, so he needed Beatrice to find out this baby's full name and talk motherhood with Inscoe's wife. He would write a memo.

"Boy, do I need a nap!" Roscoe said to himself.

"Freda! No visitors nor phone calls for one hour, please," Roscoe sighed at his secretary.

"Yes, boss you can count on me!" she said.

Roscoe would call Guy as soon as he caught up on some sleep. They slept little at Trevor and GM's, and none at home!

Debbie had Tate all to herself, "We actually have the whole swimming pool to ourselves. Can you believe how quiet it is here?" She swam into his arms and shivered.

He was loving this because the less people around the more his wife would tease him. He loved his family, but hoped they'd stay away for a few days.

"We have homework to catch up on," Tate told Debbie.

"You have not done yours?" she said innocently. "I have done all my teacher asked of me."

"I'm not talking about schoolwork. I'm talking about homework," and brought her up against him which was growing by the minute.

"Don't let that thing get out of hand. Somebody might think I have not been doing my wifely duty," she took her hands and anchored it behind her. It was rubbing her backside.

She grabbed onto the side of the pool for dear life and the water was slowly lapping at the pool wall.

"Don't please Tate! I'll not be able to hang on and I'll scream if you don't turn me a round now and kiss me," she confessed.

He could not and she put her mouth on her forearm and muffled the sound as she went over and then under the pleasure zone. Then he covered her mouth.

"I have missed our free time," Tate said.

"We both have, but I miss the family being together already. You are the best thing that has ever happened to me," she said and smiled from ear to ear. "You know we cannot come out here alone again!" she said. He nodded.

"Trevor you bought me the trike and I intend to use it so get on!" GM said. He got on reluctantly and she sped off down the long road away from Southfork.

Madeline was loving the wind in her hair. Trevor was hanging on for dear life. When he bought her this Harley

Davidson, he never dreamed she would be whirling him around these curvy roads at break neck speed. She was loving it, so what the heck.

They pulled up at GM & GS Private Investigation Service office door. She took her helmet off, and fluffed her ponytail. "This is where I get off and let you take it for a spin. I'll be here till five! So don't be late to pick me up or I will have to hitch a ride with GS on that little motorbike of his."

"Guy knew about this? Hmm … I have a bone to pick with that boy," Trevor got off and was going to open the door when Guy rode up on his motorcycle.

He parked and was taking off his helmet when he saw Trevor's face which was livid. He put his helmet back on, and just sat there. He could not run over or get around that six foot four tall Texan. There was nowhere to go. So Guy sat hoping his grandma would calm the angry man.

"What in the Sam Hill do you two think you are doing?" he asked with his stance wide and his arms crossed looking at Guy.

Madeline was pulling on Trevor's upper arm that was not budging and shouted, "We are opening up the business again. I told you that waaayyyy before all this other happened!"

She got between him and Guy. Guy just sat there astride his streamline "Lightning Bolt" motorbike with his helmet still on and with his arms crossed.

He had his Kaiser sling-blade knife up his sleeve and a Luger 9 mm in his back holster … with ammo in each coat pocket. Just like the olden days when he came to this office.

He had no ammo against Trevor that he could use. He loved the man. So he would wait and see... how GM faired... before he got off.

She undoubtedly forgot to tell him about their joint venture to reopen the business. She had drove him here. Guy deduced, so she knew it would be a confrontation and she was probably counting on him to smooth out the wrinkles with Trevor.

"Here we go," Guy said to himself and got off the bike. He took his helmet off and looked Trevor in the eye, putting the helmet under his arm, and walking to the front door.

"Have you got the key GM?" he asked his grandma.

She answered, "No, I thought you had it GS!"

Trevor stood silently for a good two minutes and then he said, "You two are something! Can't even get in the front door!" and he grinned and let out a belly laugh that made them both laugh.

He reached in his pocket and pulled out the key, and held it high in the air. "Is this what you' all been wanting? The key to this office. Hmm … I knew you two would be down here sooner or later. I have kept it in my pocket every day since I bought her the trike. Guy what do you have to say for yourself?"

Guy cleared his throat as if to answer.

"I am the one that suggested it, Trev. He will do anything to please his grandma," and she blew Guy a kiss and he caught it. He then slapped it on the back of his neck.

"Does that answer your question, Trev?" GM puckered up a kiss for her husband and planted it on the side of his face.

"Don't Trev me, and not in front of the boy. Okay! This is to be just minor P.I. stuff, nothing more! If it becomes major stuff, then I get to play boss. Is that a deal?" he looked from Madeline to Guy and back.

They all raised their fists and said, "Here!Here!"

"Since that is settled, I think I'll go on home and take a nap. I'll be back at five sharp, little lady!" and kissed her ponytail.

"Oh NO you don't. Turn your head sonny!" talking to Guy and he went into the next room.

She grabbed his shoulders and hoisted herself up to Trevor's height and planted a juicy kiss on him and said, "Thanks darling. Now give me the key. We might want to lock up when we go to eat lunch," and held out her hand.

He reached in both of his pants pockets and pulled out two keys. "I'll save you the trouble dear, of having an extra key made. This one is mine and this one is yours." He handed her her key and she blinked, "You are amazing Trevor. Always one step ahead of me!"

"This is true! When I married you you hesitated on OBEY, when you repeated love, cherish, and obey. Nothing gets pass me!" and Trevor smiled. They heard Guy laughing loudly through the wall.

Roscoe was still assigning the security for all the family 24/7. Marcus was keeping his men here in town to secure his home, but he asked to have Roscoe's security team hired ... one for THE HOTEL & one for THE CASINO 24/7.

This meant Roscoe's security business was booming, and he was going to have to recruit more employees. Today he was going to have a big meeting, and he had asked Beatrice not to come to his office for any reason!

Roscoe's men were the best, and he shook each one's hand as they came into the conference room. "I have a lot to discuss today, but FIRST … I must thank each and everyone of you for keeping my family safe during this trying time. You are the best!"

He clapped for them as did the clerks and all personnel that worked there who were not guards. "To show my appreciation there will be a little something extra in your pay this week. No! It is not Christmas!" a roar of laughter.

"But speaking of Christmas I have to ask for my present this week." He paused and marched to the chalkboard and wrote:

I HAVE TO CLONE THIRTY TWO OF YOU FOR TWO NEW JOBS!

"What does that mean? It means we are expanding our coverage and I need you to talk, call, and beg only the best! People you know that could handle a hotel and casino security position," he paused. Then began pacing the room.

"Any grandfathers, cousins, nephews, brothers ... or sisters that are trained and dependable ... send them to see me!"

He put his hands on the table, and looked around and smiled. "For each recruit that passes inspection, there will be a $100 bonus for whom sent them. Sound good, guys?"

It was a roar heard all over town. The police department was calling to see what was going on. Freda said, "I cannot say! It is a secret. BUT if you can come over, Roscoe will tell you!" she quickly hung up because Roscoe was walking her way.

"Did I hear my name?" he was eyeballing her and she was grinning like a Cheshire cat.

"Freda what did you do?" Roscoe asked coming around the desk to stare at her.

"I want my hundred now! I have the entire police department coming over to talk to you!" Freda said and held out her hand.

"Is that a hundred for each one that signs on?" she questioned and laughed. "Forget that boss! I wouldn't know what to do with extra money!" She laughed and went back to typing a report pausing to answer the phone.

"Smith Security … may I help you!" and she smiled at her boss that was just reaching his office. Where his lovely wife was sitting on his desk. Her favorite tie was around her neck, and her legs crossed with her lips puckered. Roscoe locked the door and pressed the intercom button, "Hold my calls, Freda!"

"Why may I ask have you come to my office today dear?"

"Because you forbid me. I thought maybe you had a woman hid in your office to play with and I was going to scratch her eyes out!" Beatrice smiled and placed the tip of the tie in her mouth.

"Do you realize how many people are outside my office and the police department is on its way?" Roscoe sighed.

He walked to her, and escorted her to the private bathroom in the back of his office. She was strutting in those three inch high heels that he loved.

"You my dear will have to sit on that throne until I have finished hiring thirty two people. If you move, we will not be able to afford those TRIPLETS that will be born nine months from today. Is that clear?"

She was taking her lacy panties off, and putting them in her purse and unzipping his pants because she knew him well enough to know, he could not wait that long!

She said as he sat her on the sink, "Crystal clear! Now get on with the program mister! My husband may come in any minute! Yes you are the best thing that ever happened to me. I will never tell my husband that he is missing a tie from his wedding suit! If you just ... just .. Oh Baby!"

CHAPTER THREE

Corey and Ellen were redecorating his room. He told her to do whatever she wanted to do with it.

Eunice said from the laundry room, "I have begged him to paint the walls Ellen. You have my permission to paint them pink?"

Corey was jumping up and down, "Don't listen to her Ellen I beg of you. NO PINK!"

"Sounds good to me," answering Eunice's choice. Which both the women knew, they were joking.

Jason came by Corey and patted him on the back, "Hot Pink I heard through the grapevine."

Corey looked devastated. "I'm taking you to Lowe's now and we can pick out a color together that is not pink."

Ellen nodded, "That would be great!" They climbed on his motorbike and off they went.

Corey was still working for Roscoe mopping floors part-time, but he was going to ask for a permanent job this week.

He could go to school at night once a week.

They picked out a pale blue and Corey was ready to paint and so was Ellen. They stripped the room, and started in on the chore. "It is fun to do stuff together, but I can hardly wait to get these paint clothes off. Go lock the door."

"No ... your mother is here. Are you crazy?' Ellen said.

"Yes over you. They left to go to the store ten minutes ago. We are wasting time. Baby! That is it! You know..."

They had paint everywhere, but on the walls. Corey was busy taking paint remover to the floor and Ellen was busy painting around the window sills when Eunice came back.

"The walls are looking good Ellen. Did clumsy here spill some on the floor?"

Quickly Ellen said, "Yes all over the place. It was all over the place."

Corey was still cleaning, and closed his eyes to remember what they had done to each other only minutes ago in this very room. "I made a mess!" he was staring at Ellen's buttocks as she reached high for the top of the window. Then down to the bottom stepping on the ladder just enough to jack him up again. She puckered her lips with each paint stroke.

He just stopped cleaning and went to take her in his arms. "You can't do that to me any more. I will pay you back tonight, and I don't care who hears."

"You wouldn't dare," she moved back and painted his nose.

"Mom help! Ellen is painting the wrong area," Corey said.

Eunice had a grocery bag in her arms and looked in, and saw he had paint on his nose and said, "That's an improvement Ellen! But he still has to get it off the floor. Marcus is coming for dinner. So get it done. Get it done now!"

They were dressed and paint free. They had scrubbed each other clean, and dressed with care because Marcus would be hiring at his hotel. Maybe they could both get a job there.

Marcus may consider him for any job. He would ask about the training for his jobs and where to apply? She would, too!

Adriana and Unitus had not told anyone about the baby. She was working on several cases. Her time was limited. She was getting the best foot massage from her loving husband that had made a casserole which he actually knew what was in it!

He got it off of the internet with step-by-step instructions, and he had fed and bathed their daughter. She was playing in her new jumping chair watching her daddy rub her mommy's feet.

"She will be walking soon. Look at her moving it!" Adriana was so excited. "She can get everywhere. Oh my goodness your fingers are making me. I must get out of this dress."

"Allow me," he pulled it over her head, and she sat in her lacy lingerie that Jana had helped her pick out.

Unitus was not expecting that. She never had anything frilly on, and he was so turned on. He scooped her up, and had her on the bed when he thought about Angel and the casserole.

"Don't you move!" pointing to Adriana. He went and sat the casserole on the counter, and got the jumping chair, and flew to their bedroom cutting on the cartoons.

He undressed and slid in the bed beside her and she said, "My you have missed me today! O darling it is so so what I need!" and he pleasured her as the baby bounced. They rocked it except it wasn't ever one time but multiple times for them. Eventually they put Angel to bed because she was asleep in her chair. They turned the monitor on, and sat in the kitchen eating at one AM, the warmed up casserole.

He said, "I am getting Angel used to running in her jogging buggy."

Adriana frowned, "I am sorry this situation at Trevor's has messed up your training. With another baby on the way, I need you to be safe, and not chance injuring yourself. I know I am being selfish. I can't do anything by myself anymore . I need you all the time. I rest my case."

"How about you stop working and I train?" Unitus asked.

"I have a commitment. I know I want it all. You have given up so much for me," she was agonizing over what she had taken from him.

She had tears in her eyes, and Unitus kissed them away. "Don't you dare do that! You are worth everything to me. I give you my all. No more will I ask. We will work it out. No tears please. I cannot handle that!"

"Honey! It is just hormones! That is all! Now make me smile and I guarantee, I will cry with joy!" and she laughed as he picked her up, and laid her on their bed.

He went and checked on Angel and she was sleeping. Then Adriana was sleeping. He lay and looked at the ceiling.

They were going to have another baby. Wonder if it will be a boy? They had to plan. He had to set a new goal for his life.

Adriana was right he was lawyer material. He was going to check into a refresher class. A two lawyer family would make enough to come off this mountain with two kids. He needed to be on flat ground where he could run after them better.

Adriana would understand, but she loves it here so... and so did he. Bruce will listen to him and give him advice. Sleep!

Eunice had the table set and in one of her new outfits. Cassie had fixed her hair and she was looking forward to Marcus coming to her humble abode.

Jason had made himself look quite the well dressed thirteen year old. He had styled his hair like one of Ellen's magazine male models this week. Several of the girls at school had commented on how good it looked, and how they liked it.

This year was beginning to be awesome and Junior High was packed with the cutest girls. He had never seen them in grammar grades. He guessed they were there, but he wasn't into girls until now. His hormones were raging is what Corey said, and he was getting sex education taught to him whether he liked it or not. That was fueling his need to know more.

Marcus knocked on the door, and Eunice answered with a smile that melted his heart. He kissed her cheek.

She said dinner was on the table, and they went in and ate a delicious southern cooked meal. It was his favorite, and she sure could cook. They let the kids do the dishes while they sat in the living room drinking coffee and talking. He asked if she would take a ride with him that he had something to talk to her about privately.

She told him sure, but she was worried. It was something bad? Or was it going to be about one of her boys? She just could not fathom what it could be?

She was escorted to the limo and whisk away to where the site of his mansion was being built. The framework of the huge mansion was complete. They got out and walked around. Marcus stopped, and reached into his coat pocket, pulled out a tiny box. He opened it as he went down on one knee, "Will you marry me Eunice?"

Eunice was shocked, her legs were about to buckle, but she stood still as possible.

He steadied her, "Well?"

She swallowed as she thought, looking at the sky saying to herself "this can't be happening what should I do?" then she said.

"Yes ... I will marry you on one condition!" Eunice said.

He looked puzzled, "You want a prenuptial?"

"No, I just want you to promise to try not to change me. I am comfortable being me, and am not a fancy woman. Can you promise me that Marcus? If you can, I will be your wife."

"I love you exactly like you are. No one had better try and change you, or they will have to deal with me."

He took the ring out and slid it on her finger. It fit and he kissed her, and she swooned. He was being so gentle with her.

She had witnessed how rough and tough he could be with others, especially in the business world.

He knew he was going to have to tread softly in order to get this woman to trust him. She felt so perfect in his arms like no other had ever felt, and he had had some beauties.

Eunice was beautiful inside and out. He was a happy man. She had said, "Yes."

They went to her house. She showed her ring to the boys and Ellen. She could not stop smiling at Marcus.

Marcus and Eunice were going to make their rounds. Trevor and Madeline's was going to be their first stop. They were so happy for them. They called to see if they could stop by Adriana and Unitus's, and they were home.

"We have some news to tell you!" Marcus said.

Adriana said, "We have some news to tell you!"

Eunice walked in, and showed them her ring. Adriana hugged her, and then her daddy.

Marcus said, "Okay! What's your news honey?"

She turned to Unitus, "You want to tell them?"

He walked over, and began to rub Adriana's tiny stomach.

"I think it is a boy!" Unitus shouted.

Marcus and Eunice were hugging them. "That is wonderful!"

Adriana said, "You two are the first ones that we have told."

"Unitus my boy, you have made my little girl so happy! I have never seen her smile so much!" Marcus sat beside Eunice on the couch.

Adriana growled. Unitus smiled, "Gas pain, dear?"

Her eyes got big as saucers and she said, "I can't believe you said that."

Unitus 's retort was, "That's what you say when Angel makes that face!"

Marcus by now had Angel on his knee and she was wiggling to get down, "Dada Dada."

Angel's legs were wobbly, and she was holding Marcus's finger. Then she let go, and steadied herself. Then took her FIRST step, and then another, and sat down with a plop.

Adriana ran for her, "My baby! Get the camera and maybe she will do it again. I want to write today's date on the back of it."

Eunice said, "She is getting out of the way for her brother." They all laughed and agreed Angel would be walking, if not running by the time the new baby came along.

Adriana asked, "Have you'all set a date?"

Marcus said, "I just asked her dear, and it will have to be after the house is finished. Unless we can move in with you and Unitus?"

Unitus was shaking his head, "Sir, I cannot let you take away Adriana's bed, and it is the only king-sized bed my body will fit in," he was stammering. Adriana was rolling her eyes at him.

"Okay you can have our bed. We will just have to sleep on the sofa and watch the sunset over the mountains. Excuse me! I have to go change the baby," he grabbed Angel and walked very fast to her room before anyone could see his boner.

"Thanks, but it will be awhile before we decide. It was sweet of you to offer," Eunice said.

Adriana shouted, "Honey don't pout we can sleep on the sofa tonight anyway!" She had seen what the mention of sleeping on the sofa watching the sunset had done to her husband. She also was remembering the first night here and she probably was blushing herself.

Marcus asked, "Where will the new baby sleep?"

Adriana answered, "We really haven't thought about it. Hmm I can't bare the thought of moving off this mountain. I love it here in this spot." She frowned and whined.

"I understand Adriana. It is beautiful up here!" Marcus had walked to the window and was enthralled by the beauty of the mountains. At the bottom was the lake gleaming in the last bit of sunshine, reflecting the trees and mountains like a mirror.

He motioned for Eunice to come stand beside him.

He turned to Adriana. Unitus was back with Angel, "I want to give the grandson or granddaughter an early baby shower gift. I will have a room added on here and your wish my darling will be complete. What do you say?"

"Unitus what do you think?" Adriana was begging with her eyes and wiggling her assets.

"That sounds generous Marcus anything that makes my girls happy," Unitus said as Angel was bucking to get down, and she went walking wobbly legged at first, and then running across the room to her mother.

"I love you daddy! Thank you! Now we can relax. It was weighing on both our minds," Adriana said to Marcus.

"When will your house be finished, Marcus?" Unitus asked.

He looked at Eunice, "Next month," he had an arm around her shoulder and he squeezed it.

"How is your training going Unitus?" Marcus asked.

"I'm way off track with this Jung thing and Adriana doesn't want me to compete. She says the two kids will be enough for me to run after." He looked at the ceiling.

"Adriana! MY child you are being unfair! This man," Eunice was pulling on Marcus's jacket sleeve.

"Eunice I have always told her the truth, and I'm not going to stop now. Adriana … Unitus is a good husband, but you got to loosen up. He is a great athlete and if you break his spirit. Mark my words, you will regret it. Unitus Son, I had already prepared to sponsor you and the vets. It has been so much going on that I forgot to tell you!" Marcus grinned.

Unitus was beaming and Adriana was sitting with a pouty mouth staring at Unitus.

"Daddy I am the ONLY one that is suppose to put that big a smile on his face," and she hugged her father.

Unitus was stuck to the spot where he stood, not believing what Mr Moneybags had just said. Adriana pinched him.

"Honey are you okay?" and all he could do was smile and shake his head yes. "Daddy has that affect on a lot of people!" she knew her daddy took pleasure in helping with his money.

Once he had told Adriana, "Why have money, if you can't help the ones you love when they need it." She took Eunice by the hand and walked her into the kitchen and shared this with her, so she would better understand her father.

"We are going to fix coffee!" and they talked and talked. Eunice felt much better after Adriana made her welcome.

"I'd rather have a martini," Marcus said and Unitus fixed it.

CHAPTER FOUR

Roscoe was busy. Interviewing the new applicants and the quota was looking good. Buchanan's THE HOTEL & THE CASINO would be completed in the next six weeks.

At least that was the projected time of completion, by then he would have each facility manned with the adequate security staffing. Freda, Roscoe's secretary had put the blueprints to both facilities in the system so Roscoe with one touch could pull them up. The sites that each had to have coverage was marked with a red x.

Roscoe and Inscoe had met, reviewed the around the clock schedule and were revising some of the protocol that they had presently. They added the requirements for these new places. The rules and regulations of running a casino was different than those of a hotel.

In the next six weeks they would meet with Marcus, and have him look over the proposals. Then they could fine tune any areas that might need beefing up.

Freda was setting up for a punch clock to be installed at each site. Once a guard punched in using his badge, the computer would have him on the monitoring screen. The guard could report through his shoulder cam anything that was unusual. He could summons assistance with the push of a button, and everything could be monitored at the main office twenty four hours a day seven days a week.

The new guards were going to have to come in and go through four weeks of training and two weeks of testing.

They would be ready for this awesome job opportunity opening in exactly six weeks time.

The applicants were both male and female. There were several that he saw holding hands. He talked to them together.

Janice Delaney and Justin Taylor were engaged and both working at a nearby town's police department. They had fallen in love and now they told Roscoe they would be able to get married with them both working at the hotel and casino. "The increase in pay will allow us to marry sooner."

Roscoe said, "I understand you are in love, but I cannot have any of my guards holding hands, kissing, etc . When you are on duty, is that clear? If I get reports, as sad as it would be, it would be grounds for dismissal. Go do your thing on off duty hours with my blessing," and he winked at Justin.

"Yes sir! Will do!" and they shook hands.

Janice was petrified at the man-talk as if she was not in the same room. She held her tongue until they got to the car.

"Not sure I want to work for this man. He did not even look at me. I am equal to any man and deserve to be treated the same." Janice was furious and pacing around the car.

"Honey he was addressing me to prevent embarrassing you, when we start to work it will be different. If not then you will have your husband's permission to let him hear a piece of your mind." He grabbed her and kissed her before she could say anything.

She was standing on tiptoe, "Aren't you afraid your superior will see us!" She was grinning and rubbed her leg between his.

"Hell no!" he drew her nearer to him. "We don't work for him yet, but if you do that again. There will be guards coming to arrest us both for indecent exposure."

She jumped quickly into the jeep and smiled. "Just testing to see if you could get it up in public."

"Oh No! You didn't say that to me," he put the jeep in gear. As they neared his apartment building, "Your place or mine?"

"I have a trip I have take Aunt Betsy to the pharmacy today before it closes!" He grabbed her arm and said. "Good try but it won't work. Aunt Betsy was at the drugstore yesterday when I made rounds."

He was staring into her hazel eyes and that long blonde hair that always stayed in a bun under her police hat was flowing down her back in a million curls from the wind whipping it in the Jeep on their ride home.

"Okay! Your place is right in front of us. We have to talk about getting married that way in six weeks, we can keep our hands off each other." All the time he is walking he was unzipping his pants and pulling her along. In the hallway he was unzipping her pants, and she was taking his shirt off and he was taking her bra off .... "I have to read you your rights Mister!" Kissing his lips and rubbing that same leg between his as she did in the parking lot earlier.

"Jan you have the right to remain silent. Any thing I say will be used against me. Marry me tomorrow!" She said, "Yes!"

Guy had arrived at GM & GS Private Investigation Service on his bike and was taking his helmet off when Madeline rode up on her trike.

"I see you got Trevor to let you ride that Harley-Davidson thing alone," Guy said with a grin.

"Well he was asleep when I left so... we will see in a few... his reaction. Be warned!" Madeline stated as she took her helmet off, and they walked into the office.

"What kind of business have you drummed up? I see your eyes a twinkling?" GM asked after blowing him an air kiss that he caught it, and slapped on the back of his neck.

She hung her leather coat on the coat rack and dusted her cowboy boots off. "I'm listening!"

He was reviewing requests on the computer. "We have one lady that wants us to find out who her husband is cheating on her with?" GS said looking at his grandma. "What are you doing now?"

"I'm trying to find that can of coffee. I had it here awhile back," she was slamming and banging the cabinet doors.

"I guess you are saying you left in a hurry and didn't even get a drop of Go Juice?" he asked and then laughed.

"Nope, I am fit to be tied," she said as Trevor walked through the door.

"And I'm the one that needs to tie you up and throw you over my shoulder and take you home," Trevor bellowed.

"GS he hasn't had coffee either," GM said staring at Trevor.

"How do you know?" Guy asked.

"Because I have asked him to come over to the sink and let me teach him how to work the new fan-dangled coffee pot, but no .... he says that is what he has me for," Madeline was standing with her hands on her hips.

"Well fix me a cup of coffee, Woman!" Trevor demanded.

GS was sliding down in his chair, this was not going to be the morning he had hoped to get some work done.

"I will as soon as you go buy a pound of coffee at the grocery store," her wheels were turning. "Or buy one of those fan-dangled coffee pots for here. OH MY Goodness wouldn't that be just the sweetest thing, Guy?" she smiled at the grizzly bear that was standing in front of her and gave him a kiss on the cheek.

All the while batting those eyelashes, and he turned waving at her, "I'll be right back, dear!" Trevor mumbled all the way to the car.

"The feed store was broken into, and they don't have cameras. So they want someone to find out who took their cash register," GS was reading off possible cases to GM. She didn't say anything just sat here.

"Okay are you alive over there," Guy asked.

"I'll be answering those questions after I drink me some coffee. Just keep on reading," GM said.

"What do you think about Mr Buchanan and Ms Eunice getting engaged?" GS asked his grandma.

GM said, "Eunice is perfect for him, if he doesn't hurt her. Then I'll have to kill him." GS gasped and his eyes widened.

Corey had to ask his mother and Ellen was behind him peeping over his shoulder. "If you get married to Mr Marcus can we have this house or do we have to move with you?"

"I don't know can you afford this house payment, lights, water, insurance and all the repairs. Or do you two want to move with me and Jason where the rent is free, free food, free insurance, a swimming pool, limo etc. IT is for you to choose and let me know before I wed Marcus?" and she walked to her bedroom and left them in the kitchen staring at each other.

"We pissed her off big time! What were we thinking? What was I thinking! I think we should move with my mother. What do you think Ellen?" Corey really had not thought about how wealthy Marcus was, but all he wanted was to have Ellen alone all the time.

"Corey we would be stupid, if we didn't go with your mother. We need to be there for her so she will have someone she knows to talk to. She will not have to work and she does keep going to work," looking out the window at Jason skateboarding on the porch.

"Corey tell Jason not to skate on the porch please. He scares me! Yikes, too late! He bit the dust!" They ran to see if he was hurt.

Eunice went running and took Jason to the hospital, and sure enough he had broken his left arm, and they cast it.

Jason was home for a few days and said, "Everyone will run to see it! All the girls will want to sign it. Guess it is a chick magnet!" Corey looked at Ellen and just shook his head.

Beatrice had bought a four-seat stroller, but it was too hard for her to handle. Roscoe fixed Dynamite up with a harness and voila. She was able to go over to Kyleigh's without any problem.

The kids were strapped in and giggling when they arrived, Kyleigh and Madison ran out to meet them. Madison said, "I want to ride." Beatrice and Kyleigh looked at one another and was able to seat him on the back rack.

Kyleigh said, "I want to ride."

"Stop it! I need you to help me steer this thing and keep that dog from running after Velvet."

"You want to let's take them down to the lake and see how the boathouse is coming along?" Kyleigh asked.

"Sounds good. It'll just give the nanny a break and Mrs B is fit to be tied," Beatrice admitted.

The walk was good for the mothers to get out in their skinny jeans and enjoy the sunshine and fresh air.

"The house closes in on me sometimes," Beatrice was sighing. "But I would not let Roscoe know that. He is working so hard. I want him to think all is peachy, you know what I mean?"

"Yeah we have got it made, they think," they both laughed.

"Will you look at THAT!" the boathouse was completely done.

"They finished it and didn't even tell us!" Kyleigh was gazing at the detail. The large porch wrapped around and the railings were high and kid friendly.

"The kids can get out and run around inside and out without fear of them falling over," Beatrice was in awe.

They let the dogs loose to play and took the babies out and walked them carefully into the boathouse.

"It is beautiful!" the fireplace was massive and the ceiling had all exposed beams. "I bet Roscoe and Guy could put some swings for the kids on those beams, if Trevor will let them."

"We can come down and have cookouts soon. What do you think? We have to call Madeline now!" and they did.

Guy said, "This is not a good time darling. She and Trevor are discussing a coffeepot!"

Kyleigh said, "Let me talk to your grandma."

Guy said, "No, dear. Not today. I will explain when I get home," and he hung up.

Kyleigh looked at the phone and looked at Beatrice, "He hung up on me!"

"Oh my Goodness … What do you think is going on?"

Guy had gone out into the yard and called Kyleigh back, "Sorry hon, I could not talk! They are having a fight. I think, and I didn't want to interfere. So what's up?" he kissed the phone.

"That's better! Don't you ever hang up on me, darling?"

Kyleigh smiled into the telephone and showed him Beatrice's scowling face. He understood that he had embarrassed her.

"Sorry honey. It won't happen again. Girls what are you two doing? Where are the kids? What do you need GM for?"

"Whoa, baby! One thing at a time. Let me show you," and she turned the phone around and scanned the boathouse. It was filled with the kids playing and the dogs barking. Dynamite came and licked the phone.

"Awesome I want you to do that ... OOPS! Sorry Beatrice I was thinking out loud," GS said.

"That's okay! Sounds like something your brother would say," she admitted and he felt better.

"Wonder when they finished it?" Guy asked.

"That's what I was going to ask GM and find out when we could have a cookout. So when they fix that coffeepot find out for us and let me know tonight. That is … if we ever get all these children back up that hill!" the girls both laughed and made faces into the phone.

"Love you! Bye Baby, see you tonight!" Guy hung up and Kyleigh kissed the phone.

"Didn't want him all hot and bothered! If I kissed the phone before he hung up, he would be home and spoil our day out!"

"Good thinking sister! Sounds like his brother!" Beatrice said. They went to change the babies, and talked and talked.

The housekeeper and nanny had the house clean and supper started. They actually welcomed Beatrice and the four children home. The dog went straight to lay by the fire.

"Dynamite looks exhausted," Mrs B said. "He is not use to playing with the kids and Velvet all day!" Beatrice said.

CHAPTER FIVE

Tate and Debbie were meeting at the library after classes. Tate was really doing well in his criminal justice classes. The business classes that he took last year did not interest him like this did. He had a passion for detective work and wanted to follow in Guy's footsteps.

Roscoe was encouraging him. Debbie was his biggest cheerleader, and Mr Marcus's statement to do what you love, nail it on the head for him. He had sunk his teeth in and was excelling in his schoolwork. He loved it.

As they met Roscoe, Tate asked him if they could swing by and get a pizza that Debbie had cooked all day, and he wanted to treat her. He called it in, and they didn't have to wait.

Rarely did they not eat with Trevor and Madeline, but it was their anniversary of their first real date and he wanted to always make her feel special on this day.

They went to their room to dine. Debbie had explained it to Madeline and she was happy for them to have their alone time.

Tate had his surprise for her in his pocket. After they ate, he brought it out. A small box and as she opened it, she cried. It was a locket with his and her pictures inside.

He put it around her neck and hooked it. She kissed the locket. It was not diamonds or emeralds, but it was more valuable to her because it came from Tate.

They made wild passionate love as they did that first night.

Unitus had not come off cloud nine since Marcus had told him that he had his money to help his fellow vets to compete in the triathlon.

Adriana knew it was selfish of her before to want him to quit. Unitus was not a quitter, but he would. If that was what, she really wanted him to do. She came first in his life and now she wanted to support him in all that he did.

They had worked out a system to drop Angel off by Jana's on Mondays and Thursdays, and off Tuesdays and Wednesdays by Kyleigh's only for the hours that Unitus needed to do his training on the cycle.

It took two hours usually, and she would watch her at night for him to do his swimming in their pool. The running he had fixed Angel's a jogging stroller, and she could watch her daddy run up and down the hills.

On Saturdays, they would pile in the van and go to meetings and join other vet families that wanted to compete. They were meeting couples that had disabilities far worse than Unitus's. They were inspiring him to work even harder for the cause.

Adriana was inspired to be more of a supportive wife and really was taking pride in her husband for his tirelessness. She for some reason had more energy with this pregnancy also.

Their sex life was becoming stronger and neither thought that was possible. "It must be your strength training. Please don't stop. Whatever was I thinking to deny you of this.

Unitus honey ... what was I thinking?" She could not get her breath. He took her over. "Don't ever stop loving me!"

Marcus escorted Eunice into the mansion. It was huge. The massiveness took her breath away. The marble floors and chandelier in the foyer that was as big as her whole house. The staircases were on both sides, and the columns extended to the third floor.

He was taking pride in showing her around, but it was not impressing her. Only the opposite, she was becoming more frightened. She could not possibly live here.

She asked, "Do you have a map? I would get lost in here and that is terrifying me. I am not one that does well when I get lost. I hyperventilate. Marcus I may pass out any minute."

Eunice was wobbly kneed and he walked holding her to the den, and sat her down. It had never occurred to him that this would frighten her. The usual response was the female wanted to see it all and see it all right now! She was so different.

"Eunice dear, I don't want you to feel uncomfortable. I must have been going too fast. We can take it slow. You can see it little by little, and you can get use to everything. Use to everything, and it being yours. When we marry what is mine is yours. I love you. Do you understand that?" Marcus said kneeling beside her chair.

"Marcus I am sorry to be such a prude and I know in my heart that you do love me ... and I, you!" he kissed her and she was feeling a little better.

"Let us just sit in this one room tonight and talk. Is that okay?" she asked.

He laughed, "Of course it is."

Madeline and Trevor were enjoying the dinner with Jana and Bruce. They were telling them of the boathouse that the girls had been by to see it. Trevor was proud of the finished product, "Just like I wanted it to be. I want to be able to walk out and fish from the dock, or get on the lake in a boat that Madeline picks out. She does like to shop!"

They all laughed. She said, "Now Trev. We know I just like to shop for coffeepots, and you like to shop for boats. So don't change the rules. I know nothing about boats."

Bruce said, "I will be glad to go with you shopping Trevor. We can leave the women here... to brew up their magic potions."

Both women held their fists in the air and shouted, "Here! Here!"

Madeline told Jana, "We can plan a shopping trip, too. What might you like to shop for my dear?"

"A new pair of cowboy boots," Jana said. "Three inch heels! Does that sound good! Bruce loves me in high heels!"

"Now you are talking my kind of language," Madeline laughed and winked at Trevor.

Both men were staring. Trevor said, "Bruce I think we had better go with these two shopping or some smooth talking salesmen might change their minds."

"Good thinking Trevor," shaking his head up and down to emphasize the importance of their supervision.

The women just sipped their after dinner coffee and smiled devilishly at the men.

Roscoe entered a quiet house, he was not sure what was going on. He walked through the house and no one came to greet him. Something is wrong, he went tearing up the stairs to his bedroom. "Beatrice! Beatrice!"

"Shhh you will wake up the babies," there she stood in an emerald green negligee.

"OH MY! OH MY! So everyone is in bed. How did that happen?" he was stammering, but really didn't want to know.

He was too busy taking his shirt off.

"We went to the boathouse and they played and played and didn't have a nap … so they are ALL tuckered out! Are you hungry?" which she knew he was starved by the long hours he had been working, their alone time had been nil.

"I am starving and I see just what I want to eat and don't you dare point to the little fridge over there!" Roscoe was beside himself with need.

"Come here and tell me more, big boy!" Beatrice got on her knees and helped him finish undressing as only she knew how.

She kissed his navel and pulled on his trousers and popped his elastic on his briefs and said, "Take them off!"

He turned and sat to take his shoes off, and she was rubbing her breasts up and down on his back.

Down his pants came ... briefs and all. "Triplets?" he said.

"You betcha big boy....oooh what a big boy!" she said.

He had her frazzled in no time flat. "Triplets?" he asked

"Roscoe shut up and give me my triplets!" and he did.

"This is going to be another Christmas to remember," Madeline said. "I can't believe Marcus and Eunice want to get married in our boathouse," she said to Trevor.

"But I am glad! She told me she needs to feel cozy and comfy when they tie the knot! Isn't that sweet?" Madeline was talking to a snoring man, and she smiled he had got her Christmas gift early.

The whole family pitched in to make the boathouse look spectacular. The mini Christmas trees were were all white with sparkles of crystal which lined the aisle to the altar.

The altar was placed before the massive fireplace whose mantle was lined with white candles of varying heights. Over the candles was a wedding portrait of Marcus and Eunice . It was six feet by six feet which almost reached the rafters. It was the first thing you saw as you came down the aisle due to the framework of rows and rows of crystals and pearl approximately a foot in depth around the picture.. The candles flickering made it magical to gaze upon.

The fireplace was surrounded by a white metal open screen ornate with small wedding bells and hearts. The arch was made to extend past the metal screen on either side and draped in white tulle wound around loosely. Fuchsia flowers were attached with baby's breath, and miniature holly ran throughout the draping.

The altar was where Trevor stood smiling and holding his Bible in anticipation of the marriage nuptials.

From the rafters three crystal chandeliers were hung for extra lightning. A dimmer switch set the atmosphere for the wedding as the night drew nigh.

The two hundred and fifty white chairs were placed in an arch on each side of the aisle of white Christmas trees.

The people were arriving and the ushers were dressed in black tie tuxes. Marcus and Unitus, Jason and Corey were dressed the same. The boys were anxiously rehearsing their part to give their mother away to Marcus.

Since Trevor was officiating, Marcus had chosen Unitus to be his Best man. Madeline was dressed in fuchsia and was Eunice's Maid of Honor.

There was a three piece ensemble: cello, violin, and bass playing the songs. Adriana had selected her father's favorites.

The bride came down the snow in a white sleigh pulled by a white stallion. Bruce dressed in the same black tux, helped Eunice out of the sleigh, and escorted her down the aisle to meet Marcus. She wore a simple Vera Wang white wedding gown and real cultured pearls and earrings that Marcus had given her at the rehearsal. Her hair was piled on her head and she wore a short veil and wore a white stole.

Marcus almost wobbled when he saw her. She was gorgeous. He said, "Just my size." He was always saying that. Ellen took Eunice's stole and sat by Corey and Jason.

It was a beautiful ceremony and the bar was open as was the catering of finger foods. The cake was beside the food table. It stood six feet tall on a round table that was covered by a Fuchsia tablecloth touching the floor. It was white and decorated with Fuchsia flowers, baby's breath, and holly leaves. All were made of confection arranged and cascaded down each tier of the magnificent cake.

They decided not to have a large dinner here. They were going to have a large dinner in their new home after they returned from their honeymoon.

He was taking her to Hawaii for their honeymoon. "Where it is warm, darling!" Marcus said to Eunice.

She laughed, "I have never even been on an airplane."

He said, "You will get use to it, darling! Where I go, you will go. Is that not right, my wife?"

She said, "I will, as long as you do not leave my side."

They had made arrangements for Corey, Ellen, and Jason to stay with Trevor and Madeline while they were gone.

"Otherwise, I will worry myself about them!" Eunice admitted.

Marcus said, "We can have none of that! So thank you Madeline," and he kissed Madeline on the cheek.

Trevor said, "May I kiss the bride.?" and he kissed Eunice's cheek.

The GM & GS Private Investigation Service had been busy during the holidays. Madeline was loving it, and Trevor was not a happy man. Guy had to be sole peacemaker unless Roscoe dropped by.

"About time you showed up!" GS was typing a report on the computer and saving it for evidence for one of his cases.

"So you are saying, you can't handle GM anymore by yourself?" Roscoe stood frowning and crossed his arms.

"Yep! That has always been the truth since we were little. It took both of us to tackle her," Guy said shrugging his shoulders.

"Well ... that is good to hear! I felt left out and all," Roscoe sat in the chair across from him.

"You look a wreck? What you been up to?" GS grinned at Roscoe because the only thing that could zap Roscoe's energy was Beatrice.

"Shut your face! I have been doing some homework as of late. Yes, I must admit … but it's none of your business. So how's that lovely wife of yours doing?" Roscoe had his elbows on the chair arms and laced his fingers as he reared back, stretched his legs and crossed his ankles.

This may take awhile and he sure hoped it did. He needed a break from work and family. Guy was the only one that could make him snap out of the funk he was in. It always happened after Christmas.

"Shut your face! None of your beeswax. Hey! I got a great idea why don't you' all come over and we can play some .... Yes since you want to hear about Kyleigh. She outdid herself this year," GS said.

"Whoa Whoa! I was just joking! I don't want to come over and watch you two on a stripper pole!" That aught to tickle his fancy. Roscoe knew they didn't have one or Beatrice would have told him. The girls shared everything!

Guy looked like a deer in headlights, "I don't think so brother," then he smiled. "That is a very good idea though. I'll run it by the missus tonight!"

"I'm just full of ideas," said Roscoe and GS threw a wad of paper at him.

Guy said, "She bought me a pool table, Bro for Christmas. So you' all come over and we can play while the women yak yak yak! But I sure do like your suggestion better. Boy, do I like that suggestion!" and he rolled his eyes at the ceiling.

"Look Bro, you might like that idea, but if you've got good sense you'd better keep it to yourself …. like I have!"

They both burst out laughing.

Trevor came around the corner, "Everything okay in here?"

They were going to mess with Trevor because Guy winked at Roscoe.

"We have decide to buy an object for our houses and we need your expert opinion!" Roscoe said seriously sitting straight up in his chair. "You tell him, Brother."

Guy said, "We are going to buy the wives stripper poles. What do you think about that idea?"

Trevor shook his head, "You two just won't do! Always you 'all are up to something!" and they all laughed.

Then Madeline came around the corner into the room, "OKAY! What did I miss?" looking from one to the other.

No one said a word just shook their heads.

"Trevvvvvor?" GM said patting her foot.

"These are your two boys today. I don't claim them," and he abandoned the ship, and walked to the fancy coffeepot to get another cup of coffee.

"Now what have you two done?" she looked worried.

"We were just playing with Trevor. He still takes us serious about everything. We told him we were going to get the wives a stripper pole. That's all!" Guy looked with his innocent puppy dog eyes at GM and Roscoe knew to keep his mouth shut.

"Is that all? I want one, too! Let me go tell him!" and Madeline strutted her cowboy boots into the next room. When she got there she put her finger to her lips, "Shhh" to Trevor, and waved him to come over to listen to the boys.

"Well that didn't pan out like I thought. Can you see grandma on a stripper pole?" Guy said.

Roscoe shook his head and arose from his chair, "Time for me to go! Been a blast as always. Miss you …... not!" and went out the door.

GM whispered to Trevor and he said, "I ordered her one!"

The stunned look on Guy's face was priceless.

Unitus had told Adriana that in September there was an Indoor Triathlon in Alpharetta, Georgia. "You swim ten minutes, bike thirty minutes and then run twenty minutes.

Doesn't that sound great? I swim here so it being indoors... will solve my dilemma about another blade."

Unitus was so excited that he picked her and Angel up at the same time, and rocked them. Just like he did when they first brought their baby girl home.

"I am getting big as a house you have to stop that. Honey I love it, but your back!" Adriana said frowning.

"Adriana think of it as weight training. You are a feather weight. Kiss-kiss, I need a kiss! You worry too much! Relax and let me rub your feet!" Angel was running around daddy and mommy.

"You want to help Angel? Okay let's rub mommy's feet," and they did until Adriana said as she writhed. "I'm going to pay you back for this," and looked into Unitus's eyes.

"I know and I have an appointment with you soon as Angel is in bed asleep," Unitus loved those pale blue eyes of his wife.

She had been working on a criminal court case and Unitus was helping to gather some much needed information.

"You thought any more about going to law school, honey?" Adriana asked not looking up from her briefcase.

"Adriana honey, I forgot to tell you I have my degree! All I have to do is take the boards," he said as if he was telling her about a casserole recipe that he had cooked.

"What did you just say MISTER?" she was staring at him and she could not believe it. She knew it was true, because Unitus would never lie about something as important as that.

He walked into the boy's bedroom that they had just finished. The much needed addition was going to make room for the new baby boy.

Unitus asked Angel, "Do you like your brother's room? Your mommy and I have to decorate it, then you will get more excited about it." Angel ran around the empty room.

Adriana was still standing in the same spot, "Don't change the subject! When were you going to tell me this bit of information about my husband? The father of my two children? The man that shares everything with his wife?"

OH no! She is patting her barefoot. That is just too sexy, and she knows I am horny. So I had better be tactful. He told himself and came around to stand in front of her.

"You never asked. You asked me, if I wanted to go back to school to be a lawyer. I recall I never answered you. Now we can agree to disagree ... if you want to … we can have mad passionate love, and then discuss it tomorrow ... or we can prolong my lovemaking to the love of my life... and we both get frustrated. Answer the question you say ... I can answer it with a simple, I did not want to be a lawyer way back then! I became interested in criminal justice, CIA stuff. I think I should go back and become a judge, and order my wife to get in that king size bed before I have her handcuffed, and placed in the slammer. Oh how I am going to slam it tonight!"

Adriana set it up for the next time the attorney-at-law boards were to be given. He waltzed in and took them quickly and scored a B+ on the written part, and they gave him an oral test because it had been so many years, which he aced.

He never felt like he had to show off in front of Adriana. Bruce knew of all his achievements. The CIA did not have any agents that were dummies.

Adriana said, "Why have you let me explain everything over the last three and half years?"

"Because I love the sound of your voice and you do it so well. You get so passionate it makes me hard. If I talk … that never happens," he grinned at her.

She could never get mad at him for loving 'her' voice what a sweet lawyer like skirting around the subject. He's good!

"Don't over analyze everything I say or I will wish I had never told you. Just kidding! There is a reason. I have thought about a two lawyer family for awhile. We would have to get a nanny and she would have to be a YOUNG woman to keep up with our two children," he said. She looked at him squarely. Her eyes were quickly dilating. Then she said, "I will call Kyleigh! She will fix you up with just the right nanny. The kind I like OLD!" Adriana smiled before she kissed him thoroughly turning his toes up.

"Now you are talking, my little baby maker! How many more do you want?" Unitus asked. "Maybe three," she said. "Then when I wake up ANOTHER!" He asked, "You're not talking about kids?" "No, I am not!" she smiled devilishly.

Eunice was terrified of most everything, but holding Marcus's hand had made her calm, and she was really enjoying the flight.

"See I told you you would like it!" He said to her adoringly.

"You are right about most things! I give you that! Just remember if you walk off and leave me standing alone, I will probably embarrass you. THAT is my biggest fear. I don't want to embarrass you Marcus," she squeezed his hand.

"Relax you cannot embarrass me, my love. I am going to be right here beside you always." His phone was ringing and he turned it off. "I will answer it when we get there. I would have left it at home, but business is business."

Eunice looked out the window and wondered where they would be staying. She finally asked.

"The Ritz-Carlton in Kapalua, Maui. It's a five star hotel that I usually stay at when I'm here. You will like it. I promise," and he patted her hand.

She looked out the window and thought this is not my kind of fun. My stomach is in knots. My head is hurting. Marcus will tire of me in no time … unless I snap out of it, and she smiled at him.

He leaned over and kissed her on her lips and she felt much better. He was enjoying teaching her about his world, and seeing the big eye wonder of it all. He had not thought about the days before he made his fortune in many a year.

He vaguely remembered what had awed him. Now everything was just mundane until this woman came into his life. She had breathed life back into his bones. She didn't care if he was penniless. She surely had no idea how rich he was.

He was deep in thought of what to do. His friends would not understand and that was good. The wives of his associates would tear her apart. They must not meet. Not to think of those crazy ex wives of his. Never was she to meet them!

Yes one thing was for sure, he was not going to let her out of his sight for her own safety. Once they were back home, she could make the mansion her own. Any way she wanted it, as long as she was happy that would make him happy.

He had closed his eyes like he was sleeping. She had said not to CHANGE her. That was going to be the hardest because she will want to learn new ways to care for her husband, and boy was he looking forward to that.

One eye popped open, and he eyed her reading a magazine. She looked ravishing in her new clothes, wonder what is under that beautiful new frock.

Hmm … he would dream awhile and soon find out.

PART SIXTEEN

CHAPTER ONE

Bruce and Jana were enjoying playing with Madison this morning. Bruce had been given a reduced sentence for his help with capturing Jung. Adriana had his time reduced to five years of community service.

After they finished spoiling his grandson, he and Jana were going by the soup kitchen and serve the lunchtime meal. They did this twice a week.

Then they would go to a movie or shopping whatever she wanted to do. This woman had saved his life. If not for her, he would have never been able to know Madison. Guy and Madeline either for that matter.

He owed it all to his beautiful Japanese wife. She was amazing. How did he get so lucky? He asked himself that quite often.

Now that he knew his fate, he could plan what he would do with the rest of his life. He could not go back to CIA work. The court stated he could not have a gun in his possession ever, so that was his career blown to heck.

Then it came to him when in college, he had an interest in Mathematics. He could teach. Could he handle himself in a school setting? Violence was everywhere, but no he could not teach in a public school.

He would check into the private schools in the area and see if there were any positions open. Trigonometry, Algebra, Calculus were all his favorites. He had obtain many degrees and expertise before the CIA would even consider him as a viable candidate.

He would talk to Jana tonight, and see what she thought. This staying under foot at the house was okay as long as he had a murder conviction pending, but not now.

He could continue the community service. All he would have to do is change the lunchtime serving to suppertime serving biweekly.

He had it all worked out in his head. He still needed to talk to Unitus, to see what he thought. Unitus shared what he was going to do also, and they fist bumped. They were relieved that they had made it through all the craziness together.

"Good friends are hard to find!" both said it at the same time. Then they went their separate ways to meet their wives for supper.

Jana told Bruce I think it is wonderful, if it is what you really want to do. I will be here waiting for you to come home. She was hoping that he was not going to do anything stupid. It was his decision. He had lied to her before, but it was to protect her. This sounded legit. Time would tell.

He was in luck. A math teacher position was open at the Jackson Private Academy nestled in the Blue Ridge Mountains. He applied online and for the 12th grade slot.

Tate and Debbie, and Corey and Ellen went to the movies together. So Jason had one of his friends named

Charlie over to spend the night at Trevor's. Madeline helped them roast marshmallows in the fire pit and made Smores.

"Boys I have been trying to get her to do this for years," Trevor said. It was snow on the mountain and sitting outside around the fire pit made it warm and cozy. They sang campfire songs and Trevor told them the gosh awful ghost stories.

The boys were playing on the XBOX when the couples came home. "BRR … It is cold out there. It was fun to go out. We will say goodnight," Tate said as he ushered Debbie quickly to their room.

Corey and Ellen waved at Jason, "Goodnight all!" and they rushed to their room.

The movie they had seen was very provocative and a X-rated movie. They did not think pass the front door just how FAR actors and actresses went in sexually explicit scenes these days. They all did not look to the left or the right while in the theater. The girls saw things they had never seen before.

Both the girls' brows were raised, "OMG!" "I can't believe this!" Ellen was really into it and Corey knew it. She was squeezing his hand so tightly. Which it had a different effect on Debbie. When the actor held the actress down and took advantage of her, she turned and looked into Tate's eyes. He said, "I didn't know! Do you won't to go?"

"No, I will not spoil anyone else' good time. I have to get past it. You will pay when you get home." She did not say the payback would be good or bad. So Tate watched the movie and it had a happy ending, and he hoped he would, too!

Corey told Ellen that he was going to talk to Jason, and she whispered, "You can talk to him tomorrow. Don't interrupt the flow of my juices." He stepped up his strides to almost a run to their room pulling her along. What a difference a few choice words could make!

Tate and Debbie were in a strong embrace and he was kissing her neck and apologizing. She was pulling his shirt out of his pants and over his head as he did the same. They had not had time due to school and homework to have any alone time. The movie made them horny as all get out … so the bare breasts were just a tease for what was to come.

Debbie unbuckled his jeans and caressed all she wanted, and she knew, it was all hers. His pants fell and he kicked them to the side.

Tate undid her wrap-around skirt, and it fell to the floor. He eased her thong down a little so his fingers would have free rein.

She said, "I have missed you so much … oh that feels so good!"

She eased his briefs down a little and fondled him.

"That's it, I gotta!" he said and she said, "Me, toooo!"

She fell back on the bed and did not completely undress. It was no need. Everything fit so well in the right places, and he rocked her world again and again, "We needed this!" "Yes!"

Corey was asking Ellen how she wanted it, "I saw that look in your eyes during the movie and you squeezed my hand. I knew you wanted to try it. Was I wrong?"

She kissed him and turned her back to him, and dropped her corded slacks and kicked them off. She had no panties on and said, as she bent over. "I want it like that girl got it … but only if you can make it last?" She turned her head to see what he was doing. He had it ready.

"It is so... Corey, Oh baby. That's it!" and she tightened. He was counting to a thousand trying not to look at what she was doing to him. She was on her all fours by now and it was…

"Corey!"

He took her until they both went in all directions. The glory was worth the wait. She was spent, and he was holding on to her because he was still having wonderful spasms.

"Thank you for counting to 125. I heard you. You waited for me and it made the biggest organism that I have had yet!" she admitted to him.

"Oh Ellen can I turn you over?" and she did and wrapped her legs around his waist. The way he liked it best. Then he was lost and took her with him.

They did not want to go to the shower, but they had to because they had one more thing that they wanted to try.

"I can't believe we are doing this!"

"We are just experimenting that way we will know what feels the best. Being married gives us freedom to do what we need anytime, anyway, anywhere! Right?" he asked. "Yes!"

The Ritz-Carlton was a five star hotel she had read up on it and it was beautiful and their room was an ocean view. They walked to the balcony to gaze at the blue water while it was still daylight.

Eunice had worn slacks and boots on the plane trip because it was so cold back home. The balcony breeze must be a good 80 degree, she guessed.

"Marcus you know we are going to have to go shopping. I bought the wrong clothes to wear. I bet you bought just the right clothes," she said.

"I wouldn't know. George does all my packing and he hasn't let me down yet!" Marcus laughed.

"Who is George?" Eunice was anxious to meet all the staff and keep their names straight.

"He's my valet and butler. He has been with me dressing me for twenty years. The maid will do it for you from now on. That is if you want her to, my dear!"

"And what is the maid's name? I really want to know these two before I get back," she lowered her eyelashes.

"Her name is Agnes and she has been with the family for twenty-five years. It is okay, if you don't know their names right off. Don't worry you will be fine. I will be right beside you. Now what would you like to do? There is a spa. We can get a treatment and relax or we can go eat some seafood."

"A massage before supper sounds delightful, but I need to unpack first," Eunice told Marcus.

He patted her hand and gave her a quick peck on the lips.

"You are Marcus Buchanan's wife now. The hotel valet will do that for us. Now relax and let's go shopping and then get a massage before dinner. Okay?" he asked.

"Whatever you say, my husband," and Eunice was grinning at him and holding his hand tight.

They strolled to some shops and she picked out some shorts and sandals, a couple Hawaiian dresses, and sunbonnet. He ordered for it all to be delivered to their room by way of the valet service desk. Marcus insisted she get a swimsuit and cover-up, so they could sit by the pool maybe tomorrow.

Then they went to the Spa and got a Castaway treatment of coconut oil infused sea salt body exfoliation followed by a relaxing Lomilomi fifty minute massage with an aromatic moisturizer.

Eunice felt like a queen and definitely Marcus was her king. She told him, "This was a pleasant surprise."

"It's your honeymoon and I will suggest, but whatever you want to do is what we will do," she kissed him on the lips.

He said, "I want more of that. They taste like coconut."

She laughed and still held his hand in a vise grip. She was so afraid that he would disappear, and that this was just a dream.

They went back to their room and the clothes were hanging in the closet. Everything from their luggage was placed in the drawers and closet neatly as well.

Eunice changed into a Hawaiian dress and sandals, and Marcus into a Hawaiian flowery shirt and beige shorts with sandals. They were ready for dinner.

They were taken to the Sansei Seafood Restaurant and Sushi Bar. He ordered for both of them. Eunice was tasting things she had never had sushi, and it was really good. He told her some sushi is not good at some places. You do not know what a good sushi is until you eat it here. It's the best."

She giggled, "I'm like that about my bleu cheese dressing. I love it, but at some places it is just awful." She continued to taste and he would tell her what each was.

"What is your favorite? I need to know what are my husband's favorite dishes to cook," Eunice asked.

"Southern Fried Cooking, darling! That is all you need to cook for me. As we travel I will fill you in on what I like. Right now I have my eyes on my dessert," and he was staring at her. She was blushing big time. He had not seen a woman blush in over thirty years and it was delightful.

She had not been with a man in seven years so she was a little anxious. Adriana and Jana had helped her pick out several sexy negligees for her trip as well as lacy undies.

They are dear girls. Her daughters, Jennifer was a tomboy and Coraine had been a hippie bohemian dresser. Neither had worn anything frilly nor had she had the money to dress them any other way.

While raising four children by herself, she wore Dollar General brands. Better known as the cheap clothing. It worked for her, just fine.

"What are you thinking about love?" Marcus asked.

"What a wonderful trip this has been," smiling at him. She wanted to say it had been a long day, but did not want to put a damper on anything he wanted to do.

He yawned and said, "What do you say we go and rest up for tomorrow?"

"That sounds good to me!" she was fixing to get up and he told her to wait. He came around and helped her out of her chair, as he had helped her into the chair. She smiled and he placed her hand under his arm. She grabbed his lower arm while he escorted her like a lady back to their room.

The full moon was shining over the ocean past the swaying palms, and it was a breath taking view from their balcony.

He wrapped his arms around her as they stood there in the moonlight. "I love you Eunice!"

"And I love you Marcus!" Eunice admitted.

While she was readying for bed, Marcus was pretending to go over some paperwork. He was a little anxious because in his past marriages, he did not have to do any work in the bed-room. The women were always experienced, to say the least. Tonight this woman thinks I am the stud muffin.

She came out looking absolutely beautiful in a pale pink negligee that showed him that that petite little woman had a dynamite figure underneath those matronly clothes that she wore. He was already getting an erection.

They went slow and he kissed everything he uncovered, and she shivered. He was right! She was just his size and he was just hoping he could please her. She was moaning. He had.

CHAPTER TWO

Beatrice and Roscoe had just left the OB-GYN office and it was confirmed they were going to have TRIPLETS. Roscoe was elated. "Do you want to do the honors?"

"No, I cannot take all the fun away from you my love. You do it!" and she giggled.

Roscoe looked in his wallet for the phone number. He found it and waved it at Beatrice.

He dialed and they had the phone ready for the Skype and the nurse answered the phone.

Roscoe and Beatrice said in unison, "Surprise! Surprise! You said to call if we were going to have us some triplets. So guess what?" Roscoe was beaming and put a fake cigar in his mouth.

"Oh my Lord. It is you two. Congrats! When do I plan my vacation and then cancel it … because I would not miss this for the world. Wait until I tell the girls. I am so happy for you!" She was not even taking a breath.

Beatrice said, "In four and one half months …. we will be at your doorsteps!"

The nurse was jumping up and down. "I won the lottery! We had a bet at work. They said no way, and I said

I have faith in your husband Mrs Smith!" she was laughing so hard.

Beatrice said, "I did too!" and they laughed together.

Poor Roscoe, "I'm glad you two thinks this is funny because I have to tell the family." The nurse said she would be there for this birth with bells on her shoes.

"See you then!" and she hung up.

"Can you believe those women?" Roscoe shouted." They had a bet I would impregnate my wife with triplets. Isn't that just the best compliment EVER?" He began grinning.

"Yes dear! They know we do it all the time and that your little sperm friends are wiggling as we speak. Do you want to stop beside the road and test them out?" she was playing with his zipper while they sat in the truck. The famous Silverado that is where it all started at Kyleigh and Guy's wedding.

"Nah! We would get caught and what would I tell my crew that are counting on me. There I would sit in the pokey for indecent exposure in public. You wouldn't want that would you, my dear?"

Beatrice was grinning. "You are a legend now tell me you don't want some of this?" she slowly pulled her pale green dress up over her thighs and he was swerving off the road.

"I guess we can go through this thicket and down by the river. Won't anyone see us with these tinted windows," he was talking himself into doing what he said he would not do. He remembered the house was full and she was so ready. He was not going to pass this up for the world.

"Honey don't! It will go off," and she stopped touching him.

"Yes you are right! Your gun is loaded. I will wait and you can decide when?" She fondled herself. Then he whipped the truck to a standstill, "You just had to do that!"

"Yep you were taking too long and I want it!" She winked.

When Eunice and Marcus touched down in Charlotte, the white limousine was waiting and so was their entourage that had followed them everywhere while on vacation.

Eunice said, "I am almost use to the men being around us and at the airports. It is extra comforting, darling!"

"Glad to hear you say that! Now that we are home, they will be with us all the same. I want to go by and see the progress on OUR other projects. Unless you want to go straight home?" Marcus was patting Eunice's leg today not her hand. She said, "Sounds fine to me!"

He had said OUR projects and that meant he was including her in everything. Even his business was ours. She teared up.

She had worked in the law firm for years and saw first hand how greedy people could be. They would come in one by one to block the other spouse from any of their business contracts and monies.

Her new husband was not of that caliber. He was letting her know that from day one. That theirs was an equal partnership, and that he was in it for the long haul.

"I am with you and anything you want to do. I am by your side. Promise me, you will never tire of holding my hand?"

Eunice was still needing his support.

"As long as you always want me to hold it, it is yours!" he was also getting use to having someone stuck like glue to him. None of his other wives wanted him around unless they were the center of attention, or unless they wanted something!

This lady all she wanted was his affection, and she had it.

THE HOTEL was complete on the outside, but inside they were finishing the elaborate details. Marcus and she walked throughout and Marcus was spouting orders. A man with an IPad was taking notes and assuring Marcus that the changes would be made. He took her to the top. It was the penthouse suite, and it had no furnishings in it yet. They could see the bare bones of the structure.

He still had her hand, and lead her to the rooftop view. It was riveting. It felt like they were walking on a cloud. The clouds were enveloping them high on a mountain. They were on the fiftieth floor and no one nor nothing could see them, and he kissed her till she went weak.

"I wish this place was finished and I would show you what a mile high was," he walked her to the elevator before he embarrassed both of them. She had no clue what he was talking about.

"That would be nice!" Eunice said smiling sweetly at him.

They went over to THE CASINO and toured it. It also had a hotel within it "for the gamblers to stay" is what he had told her when she asked.

"Oh! I just have never seen a casino. The TV shows it as a fun place. The lights are so bright and the security cameras are everywhere," she stated.

"That my dear will all be camouflaged, and no one will realize that one is above, watching them at all times. The lights are bright for that very reason, people want everything dazzling," he winked. She said, "Bedazzled!"

Their next stop was Trevor's. Madeline and he met them at the door, and gave hugs to the honeymooners. The boys and girls were all at school or college at this time of the day. So they just sat down and started talking about their travels.

Marcus and Trevor eased out and went to the den as the women were laughing loudly with their enthusiasm. They were sharing stories of places Trevor and Madeline had been. The women were even comparing Eunice's photos with the pictures in Madeline's album.

Trevor fixed Marcus a martini, and he had his usual brandy.

"I want you to see something Trevor," and Marcus raised his hand, "This is the first time that it has been free of Eunice's hand since we saw you 'all last!" and he smiled. He shook his head from side to side, "I can't believe I am saying this, but it feels kind of empty without her hand in mine. Do you think we can go back in now?" Marcus frowned.

Trevor patted him on the back as they walked back to the living room where the women were still talking non-stop.

"I have been there Marcus and this phase will pass, old boy! So enjoy it while you can. I still have days that I grab Madeline's hand!" and they both laughed.

Jason came running in and hugged Marcus before his mom, and her eyes got real big. "I guess he missed you more Marcus," and she smiled at him. One that reached his heart to know that her son had accepted him … was like an extra wedding present to her. One that money could not buy.

Corey and Ellen came in and hugged them. Corey hugged his mother first. He had truly missed her, and they had never been parted since his birth. Today was the first time this young man had realized how special his Mom was. Before today, she was just MOM.

The other family members were piling in to welcome them home. Adriana came waddling in and Unitus carrying Angel.

Adriana said, "Put her down! He still thinks Angel doesn't need to walk," and they all laughed. He put Angel down and picked Adriana up and he said, "She was just jealous because her feet hurt!" and he toted her to her daddy's side, and put her down gently.

She hugged her daddy and Eunice said, "I am so glad you two are home … because I'm going to need some babysitters REAL soon!"

Unitus was rubbing her belly because that football player in there was kicking a field goal as she spoke. He could feel the strength of that kid. "He is going to be a big one like his dad. The doc said she has to have a C-section with this one."

"Yes! Drugs this time!" and they all laughed because with Angel there was no time.

As she stood there in front of them all, Adriana's water broke. "Welcome home, Daddy!" and she grimaced. "Will you all take care of Unitus. I think he is going to faint."

Bruce said, "You are right Adriana. I think he does look a little pasty!" and that brought him right out of it. "No way could we pick him up, I had to do something. That is the best way in the past. Just call him PASTY!" Bruce grinned.

Unitus swung at him and he ducked, "See he is back to normal. Now pick your wife up and let us drive you to the hospital."

"WHOA! Take the limo and we will babysit. So take your time and call us!" Marcus said. Unitus was toting

Adriana to the limo as she was talking on the phone with her doctor.

The doctor said, "Tell that husband of yours not to pick me up this time, Adriana. I have to be able to operate this time and I will meet you at the OR."

"Okay Dr Silverstein! I will give him your message," Adriana stated.

"Honey you can't strangle the doctor this time or raise him off the floor!" she shouted to Unitus who was out talking to the driver.

"OKAY! I promise!" Unitus shouted back.

"Another thing don't you touch my nurses like last time. They have to assist me and if you are under, I cannot tell you what they might do!" Silverstein said and laughed.

"That's not funny! POINT WELL taken. My contractions are very light right now! So tell them not to worry, I will be a complete Angel this time! Pun intended!" Adriana quipped.

She hung up and screamed.

James sped up to get her to the hospital.

"What is wrong? Talk to me!" Unitus was remaining calm.

"Tell him to slow down or stop!" Adriana grimaced.

Looking into Unitus's eyes, "Our baby's name? What on earth were we thinking?" disbelief was on Adriana's face.

"We thought we had more time. Breath ...hee hee... blow!"

Unitus had to calm his beautiful wife because she was making some ugly faces at him right now. "You know I can't stand to have things unfinished. What do you think his name should to be? You will have to hear me scream again, and YOU can deliver this baby, if you don't talk up!" she was playing with his nerves. He only had one last nerve left, and he was saving it for the doctor.

"Mark Van Pommel," and eyed her for her reaction.

He was waiting, "I like it, but maybe Mark Vanderbilt Pommel. Now tell him to step on it!" she was grinning.

"James take us as safely as you can, but quickly before she changes our son's name … a dozen times," Unitus kissed his wife and held her safely in his huge muscular arms.

They heard the siren and James pulled over. The same little officer that Adriana had broke his hand on the last delivery looked in. Unitus asked, "Do you want to hold her hand?"

"No Sir! I have learned my lesson. I will escort you in, and it will be my honor MR. UNIVERSE!"

Adriana was laughing so hard Unitus was afraid she was going to have the baby right there in the limo. "The man doesn't even know my name," he said.

"Honey, he knows my name!" Adriana relaxed because the hospital had sent a wheelchair out.

Unitus said, "No thanks. I got this!"

He picked her up and walked with her kissing his neck.

"Aren't I heavy darling?" Adriana cooed in his ear.

"Just a featherweight and if you don't stop I may drop you!"

"Then what?" Adriana asked knowing his answer.

"Have my way with you woman!" looking into her eyes.

"I am a happy woman as long as you say that. I feel safe leaving you for a few days at the hands of the swooning nurses, but don't forget there are cameras everywhere, and I will use them as evidence in a court of law."

Then she threw her head back and said, "I am ready for my drugs! They will give me something? Unitus? Won't they?"

He shrugged his shoulders, "Honey they may think you are strong enough to do it without anesthesia, too!"

A frightened look came across her face and she said, "They wouldn't dare! I will SUE! Will you be my lawyer? Honey! Sugar! Honey pie! Sweetums!"

He was still walking and closed one eye and looked at her, "Only ... if no one else will do it! So relax!"

They were at the OR and the doctor answered that question, "There is no one, Sweetums that would touch your case!" and smiled as they pushed her on the gurney back to be prepped.

"He is just teasing Adriana. Don't look so worried. Concentrate on when you wake up, we will have a little boy for you to fuss over."

"Hmm ... I'll have competition!" Unitus said.

She motioned for him to come closer as the nurse strapped down both her arms and put an IV line in . . . with the ... most relaxing medicine, "You will always be my big boy to fuss over over!" and she was getting drowsy and relaxing.

Unitus went to the waiting room, he did not like it this time because he could not be there. Then a nurse came, asked him to suit up, and he began smiling! I get to cut the cord! WOW!

"Why is she not asleep?" he asked.

There was a blue drape positioned to block them from the actual surgery. Unitus almost kissed her, the nurse intervened.

"You can look BUT don't touch! Stay back there. Better someone bring him a chair encase he can't take it!" the nurse had seen big men hit the floor.

"Adriana! Honey I am here with you." She looked so helpless and QUIET. This was the longest two hours of his life. Her blood pressure was going up and down, and finally the baby's cry. The nurse motioned him over to cut the cord.

He saw all of Adriana's blood everywhere and the doctor sewing her up … and he sat down in the chair.

"Told you!" the nurse gloated. "Someone get him an orange juice … probably his wife forgot to fed him."

Unitus was shaking his head for her to shut up. Adriana's blood pressure was spiking because of what the nurse said.

He stood and drank the orange juice and let Adriana see that he was okay, and then her blood pressure went back to normal. She smiled at him. The baby by then was foot printed and weighed and Unitus told them his name. Swaddled, he lay beside Adriana while the doctor continue to suture. Silverstein said he was "double knotting everything! I'll be by to see you before I leave today. Unitus I am expecting my cigar. Congratulations! This was a much better delivery, don't you think?."

"Yes, Doc! She is grinning at us!" Unitus was amazed.

"It's the anesthesia. It will wear off and you will have her back to normal. Only this time … she can do no lifting or fighting or sex for SIX weeks," he patted Unitus on the back.

"Adriana's eyes are bulging, Doc!" Unitus was concerned.

"She's fine! I did not tell her of these restrictions. I thought it would be easier for you both ... to talk it out while in the hospital, rather than reading it in a pamphlet. Some husbands forget to read them! Gotta run..." He was out the door and onto the next case. He was lagging and making small talk, just to make sure Adriana's vitals were stable before he left.

Unitus went with her to the Recovery Room. When his beautiful wife was asleep, he stepped out to get a bite to eat and have a cup of coffee.

He made the promised phone calls and talked to the family, and in exactly two hours he went back in. They were trying to get her to stop yelling, "Unitus"

He was at her side. "I'm here! It is all good! We' ll be going up to your room any minute!" and both nurses were nodding.

She wanted him to hold her, "The tubes baby! I can't right now," and she started crying.

"Are you in pain?" he was beside himself.

"No, I am good. These are happy tears. We have a son! Darling when you weren't here, I thought something had happened to him." He kissed her saying, "He's fine!""

CHAPTER THREE

Tate was graduating and on his college diploma was Tate Alexander Porter. He did not know what would have happened to him, if it were not for Roscoe and Trevor. His name had been Shackleford and only his adoption had THAT name on it.

Adam was out of prison and at his brother's graduation.

Tate told Roscoe, "I have to find out what he is planning."

Aunt Eunice was anxious and walked with Tate. They squared off with Adam, "What's up?"

"Just wanted to see my little brother. Proud of ya. You did good! Auntie you did better!" and Adam grinned.

"Not for you to worry. I'm leaving just wanted to hit you up for a loan and I will be gone!" his beady eyes were eyeing Eunice's rings.

Eunice turned and found Marcus and was shaking like a leaf. She whispered in his ear and he went and got Trevor. She returned calmer, and Tate was keeping Adam talking. He had learned that in school.

To keep the lines of communication open at all times and the outcome would be a better one.

Marcus and Trevor arrived and Adam was backing up.

Eunice said, "You are my nephew and may need a job. Is that true?" Adam was stunned.

Trevor nodded. These people that he had tried to blow their elevator up were going to help him get back on his feet.

"Why?" Adam wanted to know.

"Because you are Tate's brother, and he believes that if given a chance YOU can turn your life around," Trevor said. He was not going to trust this young man.

"You will have to prove yourself before I will ever let you near my family. Tate knows that. It is your call, what'll it be?"

Adam said, "You people can't be for real?"

Tate said, "They are Adam, come on and dive in like I did. They mean what they say. I know it is different. You have been through so much. You took care of me, so I want to take care of you! Just until you get on your feet."

Adam looked at the ground and shook his head. "I have done things to survive that I am not proud of … and I know Tate is not proud of what I have done." He turned in a circle and wiped his face with both hands as if he wanted to make sure this was not a dream.

"I have people that will not leave me alone. What do you suggest I do?" he was going to lay it on the table. Adam looked at Trevor.

"They will leave you alone ... Or they will answer to me!" Trevor offered.

Marcus said, "See these fellows behind me? They will take care of them Adam. Your aunt has told me what a hard time you and Tate had coming up. Don't think I haven't dealt with people like that before. I applied myself and I did well. You can apply yourself and do well. What do you say?"

"You got a deal!" he shook Marcus's and Trevor's hand.

Roscoe walked up with Guy, and they both recognized Adam. The faces were NOT happy faces, but they saw Marcus and Trevor shake his hand. Tate was smiling so they relaxed a bit.

Marcus said for one of his men to take Adam to THE HOTEL and get him a room, and he would meet with him tomorrow about a job.

No one was going to allow him in their house until they had seen him prove himself.

After he left, Debbie ran to Tate and hugged him. She was so frightened that the family would bring his brother back to the house, and now she would relax. She had heard from Tate some of the evil things his brother had done.

The others did not know how bad he was in the past, or did they? Madeline hugged Tate, "I am so proud of you. This is your night and we are all going to THE INN and celebrate."

Guy told him, "Now that you have your degree, you can come and work with grandma and me."

Trevor said, "I got a better idea. Tate, you and Guy can run GM & GS Private Investigation Service, and Madeline can come home to roost."

Madeline rolled her eyes at Trevor and said, "That's a possibility. If you play your cards right, mister!"

Marcus and Eunice were shouting with the rest of them, "Here! Here!"

"You have done us proud Tate!" Roscoe said.

"Roscoe, you believed in me! I thank you from my heart!"

Adam was lying back on the bed after a hot shower and had on a plush complimentary robe. He could not believe that last week he was on a cot in the bowels of hell!

"What these do-gooders don't know, won't hurt them," he said to himself and grinned. He'd play along until he got his plan together ... or then again their plan may work. We will see which one he liked best.

What he didn't know was there was a guard assigned just to him, and cameras were everywhere, watching his every move. One false one, and he would be sent back to prison swiftly.

He had seen a woman in the office that had him all aroused. He had to find out her name. I will just lay low and pounce when the time is right. For tonight he'd watch a little TV and rest up for her.

Tate spun by with Roscoe the next morning, and took him to breakfast. The boy is really trying, Adam thought and this Roscoe was making him feel at ease.

"We got to go shopping and get you some new clothes," Tate was saying as they were eating the complimentary breakfast.

"This hotel has a shop? You ain't got to do this brother,"

Adam looked at the waitress.

"I want to! You clothed me for all those years. So it is fitting that I do the same," Tate said in a matter-of-fact way.

"Okay, it's just I can't get a job looking like a hobo. I'll pay you back," and they laughed. There had been many a day that they looked like two hobos.

Madeline had text Unitus about Tate's brother, and wanted him to tell Adriana the situation with Adam. She had talked to all the women, and Debbie had talked to Ellen.

"The men don't trust him around the women because he has been in jail so long," Debbie said. Ellen nodded, "That can make a man a maniac, and boy do they want sex!" Ellen laughed. Debbie did not, and she needed to tell Ellen why.

"Has Corey ever talked to you about Coraine?" she asked.

"No, he just said his sister died," Ellen admitted.

"Well she died because she was gang raped, and she could not live with the pain. So she committed suicide. She was my best friend," Debbie said as if she was reading a newspaper article. No emotion. Ellen gasped and held her mouth.

"I was gang raped too, with her. Only Tate saved me. He is my hero. So when you talk about men that are sexually starved, I do not laugh. I am afraid of him. I don't even know him, but I am afraid of him. I cannot tell Tate because it is his brother. Please don't tell Corey I told you, but I just needed someone to talk to," Debbie stopped and hung her head. She had been so happy. Now this!

Ellen hugged her, "You talk all you want. I am here for you!Thank you for telling me that explains your reaction at the movies."

"You should have told me," Ellen repeated. "I'm sorry!"

"I got pass that because it was not real. It was just a movie.

I talked myself into not feeling! Not feeling any thing is so horrible. I feel. I still hurt! That will never go away!"

Madeline and Trevor met Eunice and Marcus to go and see the new grandson.

Marcus was overcome with emotion when Adriana said his name. He turned and buried his head on Eunice's shoulder.

She said, "It is a beautiful name. Your father is delighted."

He turned and kissed his daughter and shook Unitus's hand.

He said, "Thank you my children. We are here for you. I have very little babysitting experience as you know Adriana, but it is never too late to learn new things," and he looked at Eunice and smiled.

Mark Vanderbilt Pommel was brought in for his breast-feeding, and Unitus was devouring the sight of his son nursing his wife's breast. A tear fell from his eye and only Adriana noticed. She blew him an air kiss.

The grandparents left soon after and Unitus was able to take his son, and gaze upon him and he said, "My darling we do good work! He is very handsome!"

"He is handsome like his father that I will have to keep my hands off for six weeks … guess what the nurse told me today."

She was having a hormonal meltdown, "What tell me," as he rocked the baby. "That I can't take birth control pills, if I nurse. So in six weeks, I can get pregnant again." She wanted to see his reaction.

In true fashion he said, "So be it! We are definitely having as much sex as you can handle after six weeks."

"Adriana! Honey we had sex before you left the hospital last time," and he grinned.

"Relax! I know and you know we will never last six weeks. Am I right?" he held their son up close to her and she rubbed her husband.

"Oh that is your mommy being cruel Mark Van and I wish she would rub a little higher!" and in walks the nurse to get the baby. He looked at Adriana for help.

"Can we just keep him a few more minutes?" Adriana begged. The baby's blanket was covering him.

"Nice … I owe you one!" and he kissed her and she was not going to make him lose it because she was having fun until the pain hit her. She had moved wrong and her suture line was aching.

"Oh my! That did it. Call the nurse. Have no fear. Your pain made it go away," and he raised the blanket and she started laughing which was the worse thing to do, and the nurse was there to get the baby.

"Grab the pillow when you laugh or cough Mrs Pommel!" the nurse said and Unitus threw her a pillow. She grabbed it and laughed. The support was helpful.

"That is a nice thing to know. Unitus it works .. so yea! We are going to support this belly and I forgot how many sutures I have, but we can have the doc put them back."

"Oh no honey! We will wait the six weeks," Unitus was so concerned . "If anything happened to you, I don't know what I would do!"

She said, "Come lie beside me, so I can sleep." He did.

CHAPTER FOUR

"Bruce they called. You have an appointment at two PM with a Mr Glen Robertson at the School," Jana was so excited for him.

"Really that was fast. Will you go with me and we can have a picnic on the side of the mountain. This will be a short job, last semester of the year. If I get the job it will mean, you can help me grade papers every night."

"I'll have homework for you and you can grade your own papers," she laughed and continued fixing the basket.

When in Japan during their first year of marriage, they would fix a basket and go to the mountains, and make love all afternoon. Was this what Bruce had on his mind?

"Do you think we will need two picnic tablecloths are one?" she asked holding a chopstick in her mouth. She used them to hold her hair bun in place just like Bruce liked it.

He stared at her, "Do you really have to ask? Of course TWO," he gave her that devilish grin. The one that meant he was going to have his way with her all afternoon. She could hardly shoved the food in the basket fast enough.

He dressed in a three piece suit, and she in a kimono that had cherry blossoms on it. It took his breath away. The memories took his mind away from his job interview.

"You really want me to miss this interview don't you?"

"I want …. want whatever you want!" she was throwing her head back and strutting to the jeep with the basket. She had brought a book to read while he was in the school.

They arrived in plenty of time and she refused to go inside. "It is too pretty of a day. I'll just sit right here."

He was inside about forty-five minutes, and he had secured the position. He was now a math teacher for this school.

She was reading with those half glass reading spectacles.

She was engrossed in the book that she was reading and he got a glimpse of the material.

"Hmm so you are going to become a birdwatcher?" he asked.

"How did it go?" and pulled her eyeglasses off and bit on one of the tips. Then letting it slide in and out of her mouth as she talked and licked her lips.

"I got it and now I may lose it! A teacher in the parking lot with an erection … is not what the faculty wants, so stop! Just until I get up the mountain way away from here."

"Oh my! Way away from here. Oh my goodness, I had better air myself out," and two miles down the road she had her feet on the dashboard and her dress was flapping over her porcelain white thighs.

"You are going to make me wreck and the people around here will remember legs like that in my jeep," Bruce said reaching to rub her legs.

"Honey you got to stop. I am so so very hungry," and she pulled her dress hem higher to reveal no undies.

Bruce bent over the steering wheel and made a turn off the road. There was a restroom on the outside of the service station and he pulled her inside, and locked the door. He was so ready that it was just a matter of unzipping and she told him.

"Let me," she smiled and took all his clothes off and threw her kimono over the towel rack and stood on the toilet seat. He kissed her and then she slid down on him holding tightly. to his shoulders, and he made it worth all her time and effect Then she was begging. "Bruce please," and he took her till he could go no more, and she was sated.

"Oh baby. You are the best!"

"We are the best. Now I'm hungrier"

"Not here! let's go!"

She wiggled and he could not move. Just gritted his teeth.

"Let's wash and go to the mountain where the bears might eat my food," she kissed his neck and whispered.

"Bruce honey, don't wear that suit to school again," she said as she straightened her dress and her hair was fixed to perfection from the contents of her purse. She sprayed his favorite fragrance on her legs, and giggled.

"Why not?" while helping her into the jeep. Breathing deep.

"Because it turns me on big time and I might hurt you!"

"Did you see them two go into the bathroom together Floyd?" the owner of the store said.

"Yes I did Ferguson and you had better start charging room rates like Motel 6!" they both hooted and hollered.

"OH I think I will remember them two because they aren't from our neck of the woods," Floyd said.

"Me, too. Can't get that Japanese woman out of my mind. She was a beauty! Wasn't she something?" Ferguson spit his tobacco juice into the cup that he was holding.

The tackle store use to be a service station and now a local hangout for the retired community. Most of the time that bathroom was usually in full demand, but not today because there was a fishing tournament going on.

The principal of the Jackson Private School dropped in to see Floyd about sponsoring the baseball team. Of course, Floyd said, "Not this year, Mr . Robertson. The missus had back surgery and the hospital robbed me blind."

"The darnest thing just happened. A man in a three piece suit stopped and a Japanese woman got out of a jeep, went and had sex in my bathroom out back. Can you believe that?"

"Well Floyd I wouldn't tell anyone else. They might get you for operating without a license," and they all started laughing.

Floyd got to thinking in his dense way, "Do you reckon they could? I don't know all of the new laws they got these days!"

"No Floyd! I am just playing with you. If it happens again give me a call, I'll take care of it for you!" Principal Robertson said still joking with Floyd.

Glen Robertson thought to himself, "I sure wish it was me getting a Japanese woman hemmed up in a tiny bathroom like that. Woo Whee I do I do! Wish it was me!" and he drove off to the next establishment.

Bruce and Jana had stopped by a nice picnic table beside the road and had their picnic. She had the tablecloth on the table and the other beside her, usually they placed it on the ground and covered themselves.

She didn't ask just spread it out on the grass below the cliff and got under the cover and removed her kimono. He took his suit jacket and vest off leaving them in the jeep, but if some-one came he would be clothed. He hoped.

Jana was really making it hard to say no, and really hard to resist and he was ready for her again. She unzipped, and that was that. Two hours later, he was putting the basket into the back of the jeep. Jana was climbing in as Glen Robertson passed his jeep. He was putting his vest and coat back on.

Glen said to himself "three piece suit. Floyd had said, a Japanese woman!" Oh my goodness! I just hired that man. He is a very lucky man! I mean he is … with a geisha like that. Why would he want to teach school? Something's fishy!"

"I am sorry Mr. Smith but I have to say that our school cannot hire you after further review. We don't have the funds, but thank you for applying. We will be in touch if funding becomes available," and he hung up.

"Jana darling! Where were we? I am so glad he called."

Madeline and Tate rode into town together. Thinking they were going to the office when she surprised him by having James go by the Harley Davidson dealership. Stopping he asked, "Something wrong with your trike?" Tate asked.

She said, "No, we just need to look around for your graduation present!"

He was taken aback, "You mean I am to pick out something from here?"

"Of course unless there is something else you would like. I have seen how you look at Guy's bike so I thought this would be a good start," smiling at him.

"You don't have to. You have done too much!" he was shaking his head. This was really getting to him.

"Come here give me a hug. I never do anything I don't want to do. This is a graduation present! You deserve something special for all your hard work," and GM smiled.

"Can I call Debbie?" Tate asked.

"Do you want her to help pick it out?" she asked. He did, so she would not feel left out. She told him anything that made him happy, would make her happy.

So they started the search. He was awed by one. Madeline could see it in his eyes that that was the one. He wouldn't say it because of the price tag. The one was an IRON 883.

Madeline had the dealer to bring it out, and test drive it with the boy. "Show him Joseph, everything there is to know about this motorcycle, and extra time would be appreciated because I want a cup of coffee!" and GM walked inside.

Trevor and Debbie almost ran out the door when they heard a motorcycle coming up the driveway. She stood there with her mouth open, and Trevor was clapping, "That's my boy!"

"Do you like it?" Tate asked looking at Trevor.

"It suits you to a tee. If you are happy. I am happy!" Trevor said and Tate hugged him, "Thank you, sir!"

"Where is GM? Back signing the papers and drinking coffee?" Trevor sighed.

"She said for me to git and show it off!" Tate said smiling.

"Sounds like her. Coffee you say," Trevor went back for his keys to the trike.

"'C'mon we have some showing off to do!" Debbie hopped on behind Tate and off they went up the long pathway from the ranch.

Trevor got on the trike and off he went.

"My dear, I heard you were having coffee with Joseph. So I decided to join you!" She was fixing his coffee just like he liked it while he was talking, and handed it to him.

"She knows me well," Trevor smiled at his adoring wife.

"She does Trevor. She said fix another pot he will be here any minute," and Joseph laughed.

"I see you are still riding the trike. Don't you want to buy the little lady one of her own?" the salesman suggested.

"That's not funny Joseph!" Trevor said looking at Madeline.

Joseph cowered back into his seat and had his eyes rolling from one to the other as he bit his bottom lip.

"Good try honey! Won't work! You are to ride behind me and hold me tight!" Trevor stated firmly.

She gave him a 'wait till I get you home' look.

CHAPTER FIVE

Adam the next morning asked at the desk where the nearest barber shop was and was told there was one within the hotel. He had had money on him when he went to prison, and they handed it back to him when he left.

To himself he said might as well do the deed. With a neat haircut and a clean shave with a Manchu mustache, he looked like a real person. Now to find himself some boots, which he found also in this hotel. He told the clerk, "This is like a mini city in the sticks," and he chuckled.

"By the way who owns this palace?" Adam asked as he left with black pointed cowboy boots. The man said, "Marcus Buchanan." That was his aunt Eunice husband's name.

"I'll be damned," he said to himself. He was definitely going to be on his best behavior. Then he spotted that same pretty woman in the office area again. She was so fine. Maybe I can get the time from her.

"It's ten thirty, sir. Anything else I can do for you?" she said. He noticed her name tag said Janice Delaney.

"Would you have a cup of coffee with me?" Adam asked and smiled with his eyes sparkling. He wanted her bad, but he was going to play the gentleman.

"Sorry we are not allowed to fraternize with the clientele. It is against company policy," and she smiled and added, "but thank you for the offer."

Her smile about undid him and said, "Maybe next time you will change your mind," walking off and ran right into Tate.

"Man you look better. How do you feel?" Tate asked.

"I slept like a log. You want some breakfast? It is free called continental or something … comes with the room. You paying for my room?" Adam asked as they sat at the table with the plate they had fixed.

"Not me. Aunt Eunice's husband, Marcus. He is a swell guy, Adam. If you play your cards right and keep your nose clean, he will probably give you a job here and set you up in a room here permanently." Tate was talking and eating and Adam had to just sit, and digest all that his little brother had just said.

"You mean he will give me a job?" Adam was in shock. With his record, no one would give him a job.

"Yes Aunt Eunice believes in you, and so do I. Please Adam don't let us down," Tate was looking at him for any signs of the old Adam. He could always tell, if Adam was telling a lie.

"It is all new to me, Tate. Just give me time to adjust," he was looking at his plate.

"That is fair and understandable. But you remember Bro, I know you. If I see you getting off track, I will call you on it," downing his orange juice

"Sounds fair. What am I to do until I get a job?" he asked.

"Just take it easy. Rest up. Maybe walk around town, look at it in a different way. You maybe surprised. I love the library. You might drop by, and find something to read. That is where I met Roscoe. He saved my life. You know it! Who knows you might meet someone there."

Janice thought, "That dude is barking up the wrong tree. He is cute. Justin is my only one. He is just dragging his feet.

Maybe after this job at the hotel pans out, he will do the deed. We can get married. If he doesn't, I may have that cup of coffee with Mr. Mc Dreamy. Love that little Manchu! Oh Crap! I have lost my mind."

She had to stop this daydreaming and get back to work filing in the office until three, and back here again at night.

Her night shift security job was where Justin and she would meet up. "But we cannot touch each other while at work. Shucks! I had better call Justin," still talking to herself.

"Hi honey! Can you meet me at home at three thirty? I got something for you," she told him smiling into the phone.

"What is it Babe? I'm working!" Justin was still working on the police force to finish out his notice, and working on third at the hotel in security. It was getting him down. All Janice wants to do is have sex. "Oh yes, honey! I will be there with pronto!" and he hung up.

She got there before he did and showered, and put on a new red teddy, and sprayed his favorite perfume all over her body.

He didn't not come and he did not come … finally she was worried and turned on the TV.

"Officer was killed in a shootout at a domestic disturbance call. No names are being released at this time." She stood staring at the screen unable to move. Don't panic! It can't be Justin. She called him. He did not answer. She dressed and went to the station. They met her and said, "I'm so sorry!"

Kyleigh was waiting for Guy to come home to see how Tate was working out at the office. Meanwhile Madison had his favorite book, he was reading at a fast pace for his four year old age. She sat and they read until daddy got home.

Madison heard the motorcycle coming up the driveway and he flew off her lap and ran to the door, "Daddy Daddy!"

Kyleigh was waving like Madison … something they did together everyday. Then she squatted to be on Madison's level. She wanted him to always greet his daddy, and it be a family time when he got home.

Guy kissed both of them and sat on the floor with Madison, and did the rolling and tumbling while Kyleigh set the table. They always sat at the table to eat so Madison would know this was where you talked about your day.

Guy said Tate was a big help and had taught him some easier ways to find crucial information on the computer.

"How was your day darling? I see you have a skirt on. Is that a clue?" raising his eyebrows and she rubbed her foot up his leg.

Smiling and said, "Of course it is! I am airing out the basement!" and grinned. They both knew it meant she had no undies on.

"Oh" and he took a deep breath. "And Madison how was your day?"

Madison said, "We took pictures of the butterflies and played on the swing, and ran around to see grandpa's horses. I'm tired so I want to go to bed early." He was such a little man and now was forming his sentences with ease.

He had a good grasp on Spanish also, since Kyleigh got him a preschool video. He watched it every day. She being a teacher was making sure he was well versed in all areas of education.

He was tired by the time Guy got home, and they tucked him in bed by eight which left plenty of time for the grownups to play.

Guy showered and she had already prepared the candles in their room. She walked over to him, and he pulled her blouse over her head, she had no bra on. Her breast were no longer huge. They were perfect. He kissed her.

He left her skirt on and raised her onto the high bed and the skirt fell open and he kissed her legs as he walked closer. He was walking right into heavenly territory. She was so ready and he could not wait any longer nor could she.

It had always been that way with them, the sooner the better. Some couples had to foreplay, but not Kyleigh and Guy. It was game on from the start. Then the foreplay afterward, because one time was never enough for them.

He said, "We should have taken that skirt off."

"Really? I thought it added something different."

"It is always awesome. Everything you do is just right. We fit just right. Always have my darling. You don't have to do anything different to entice me. I lust after you most when you have nothing on."

She took the skirt off.

Tate asked his Aunt Eunice if she could get Adam a job at Marcus's hotel. "He knows he won't be able to get a job with his criminal history. I told him I thought Marcus might give him a try. He did so much for me. I have to ask. If he can't, I' ll try elsewhere. I just know I got to help. People helped me."

She sat with Tate pouring his heart out and she said, "Of course, I will. I will let you know. Love you too!" and as she hung up Marcus came around into the kitchen.

"Whom do you love?" smiling he asked.

"You my dear husband, and my nephew. That was Tate. He wants to ask a favor, and so do I," she poured the coffee and sat at the breakfast nook.

"What is that dear, to give his brother a job I guess?" Marcus sipped the steaming hot brew.

"Yes you are psychic and a sweetie," smiling at him and rubbing his cheek.

"When you put it that way, how can I refuse? I was going by this morning. Do you want to come along and be my buffer, since I don't know him well?" he patted her hand then raised it and kissed it.

"Yes you are definitely psychic. I would love to. I' ll just go dress, and be right back."

She left the room to the right.

He said, "Darling it's the other way to the bedroom!"

She still had problems of finding her way around this big house.

She was dressed and they went by limo with an escort.

He was not there when they arrived. They told the desk to call the penthouse when he came in. They got on the elevator and Eunice nearly fainted when she saw this place again.

It had been bare bones. Now it was furnished like the Palace of Versailles. It was remarkable. She thought their house was gorgeous, but this was over the top.

"I see you like this transformation. Would you like me to keep this just for us?" Marcus was fishing.

"No dear. I love our home. It is spectacular. You have to realize I have never seen anything like this or where you have taken me. I am in awe everyday. It is like I am in a dream and afraid to wake you. Please be patient with me," and Eunice kissed him thoroughly.

"You do that again and you may find out what that bed in the other room feels like," and he walked to the door and she peeped in.

"Oh my goodness! It is something out of a magazine and people come here for vacation time?" she asked.

"You can call it that, but I call it rendezvous time," he winked.

She sat on the sofa, "Okay that is enough information."

"Do you want something to drink or a snack?" he walked to the fully stocked kitchenette. Waving her to come look, so she could get familiar with the rooms.

She went reluctantly and saw all the things it was stocked with. The coffeepot was the only thing recognizable. She made them some coffee. He could not bring himself to order a pot from downstairs. She was having a good time just fixing something for him, and he smiled. "Thank you dear!"

Trevor had taught him that to "always compliment the wife in everything she does! There is a big pay off at the end of the day, and they had both laughed that day, but he was right!"

The phone rang and they told Marcus that Mr. Shackleford was back in his room.

"Have him meet me in the conference room on the first floor in thirty minutes," and he hung up.

"Take your time dear, and let's drink this wonderful coffee that you have fixed," Eunice was beaming.

"It will only take two minutes to get downstairs and be sitting at the table. So relax!" Marcus patted her hand and she held onto it as they drank their coffee.

He was right it took two minutes and Adam was sitting at the table when they got there.

"Don't you look handsome Adam. That haircut suits you!"

Eunice wanted to make him feel good about himself, and she hugged him.

"Thank you Auntie Eunice that means a lot," and he half-way smiled. Staring in Marcus's direction, he said, "Congrats on your marriage, sir. My aunt looks very happy!"

"Thank you. WE are very happy! Now we need to find out what kind of job you are looking for?" Marcus leaned forward and propped on the table.

"Anything you have open, I will take. I am not choosy. I thank you for your help. No one has ever helped me. This is all new to me. I have had to fight for everything, and Auntie knows I did the best I could for Tate." He blinked and waited.

"I will get the list of jobs and you can choose. This is a ONE SHOT deal. Do well and stay out of trouble and you can go a long way in my company. If you need anything let Eunice know. Deal?" he extended his hand to Adam.

Adam shook it and hugged his Auntie again.

He went back to his room and turned on the TV and laid down on the bed.

The news reporter had a Breaking News story and there she was the woman from the office on TV. The press was hounding her for an interview.

She was the fiancee of the police officer that had just been killed. All he could see was that beautiful young woman's face crying her heart out and twice in one day, he had feelings to emerge.

He thought he had no emotions left.

He switched the TV off and sat in darkness, just like he did in his prison cell.

Tomorrow he would choose a job and he was going to be a better man.

That pretty Janice was free now.

He was going to become the most respectable employee this hotel has ever seen.

He was going to win this woman's affections, if it killed him. She has lost her lover. I will have to work hard for her.

She doesn't know it, but she is saving me from MYSELF.

CHAPTER SIX

Ellen was babysitting Angel for Unitus to go see Adriana. She was going to have to stay a couple more days because of the C-Section.

"Unitus honey, it can't be helped. I am pitiful. They won't let me do nothing. I feel pampered sh-tless!"

He smiled and said, "That's more like my baby! They have no clue that I wait on you hand and foot, and don't you dare tell them!"

"I am no fool. Tell them then, I'd have to go home!" and she grinned showing him a little leg. With her hair all piled on her head and that short nightie, he was daydreaming again.

"Okay I will tell them," and he picked her up and walked toward the door.

"Unitus honey, put me down. I was joking," Adriana shook her head.

"I know you were, but I just wanted to hold you. I missed you last night. Angel slept with me and kicked and kicked and kicked. So I have had no sleep. Can you sit in that chair for a few so I can climb in your bed? Please honey do this for me."

She kissed him and nodded. He placed her gently into the recliner, and got her comfortable.

He dove into her hospital bed.

Two hours later, the nurse was making rounds to get vital signs, and she entered the room and jumped. There was this massive male in the tiny hospital bed. She looked at his wife and walked out. No way was she going to awaken that bear. She'd be back in thirty minutes. That's all the time she could give them, she smiled and told the others. They nicknamed Unitus "Sleeping Beauty."

When the nurse went back in, he was sitting in the chair with his wife sitting in his lap. The nurse asked, "Sir can you put her back for me. The blood pressure cuff won't reach that far." It really would, but she wanted to see his muscles.

He stood and placed his wife on the bed with one fluid motion, never turning to face the nurse and into the bathroom he went.

"Oh Lord! Adriana has done it again," he had to deal with this for six weeks..

When he came out Adriana said, "I thought you had fell in!" and he looked at her with a 'laugh now, I'll get you later' look.

She quickly back tracked, "I am so sorry. I should have said, I'd do it for you Baby, and I will when I get home!" Going back into the bathroom he went with her giggling, and holding the pillow tight to her abdomen while she laughed.

She said nothing when he emerged this time. The nurse came in, and gave her some pain medicine for a ten response to how much pain she was in, on the pain scale of one to ten.

He put her back in the bed, gently rubbed her head, and kissed her. “Get some sleep. I’ll see you tonight.”

She curled up and went to sleep.

He opened the door after a few minutes. She was in no pain.

Corey and Ellen were playing with Angel, and she was running in circles laughing at them, “You can’t catch me!”

They could but it was wearing this little tyke down, and Unitus was happy to see it.

She was in the terrible twos and her daddy was ready to play, now that he had had a nap. It was beautiful outside. If he went for a jog with her, she would fall asleep and be up all night.

He asked if they’d could watch her a few minutes longer so he could do a few laps in the Porter pool. They watched as he went in the cabana and got his usual trunks, and swam twenty minutes that was his training for the day.

“Thanks guys! I owe you one. You two are a natural at taking care of a kid. Any plans?” looking at Corey.

“No way! I like giving them back to their parents!” Corey was quick to say and Ellen was fuming. The smoke was coming out of her ears, and her foot was patting the ground.

“I mean it will be different when we decide to have some little ones, but right now we got to get jobs and an apartment or a house,” Corey was sputtering.

Ellen put her hands on her hips and stated,“We are living in a mansion. Why would be want a dinky little apartment? Besides your mother said the other day, she wanted grand kids!”

Unitus patted him on the shoulder and said, “You had better get to work!” and he picked Angel up and went out the door.

Ellen was having no touchy feely from him today! She slapped him. "I'll be in the doghouse, if you need me, Hon."

Madeline came through and saw Ellen crying, and she gave her a big hug. Mother hen was there for all her brood.

"Want to talk about it?" she shook her head no and continued crying. Corey was peeping his head around the corner at a loss of what to do.

Trevor saw him and said, "Woman trouble, son? Want to talk about it?" he shook his head yes.

"Let's walk down and see the horses," Trevor waved to Madeline to let her know where they were going.

"Mr. Trevor I don't want kids right now! She does! What am I going to do? I am too young and too immature to have children. At least, that is what I have heard people say. Then the same people tell her … they want grandchildren! That doesn't make sense! Then the big guy goes and tells her today that we would make good parents, and got her going all over again. I need some advice Mr Trevor. Big time! What do you think I should do?"

Trevor had been nodding. This boy was full to the brim with questions and had no father to turn to. So he was going to impart some wisdom as best he could.

"The thing is to let her talk it out like you and I are doing. Women like to talk, but they really love it when you listen to them. That means look right at her son, even if you had rather watch TV. Make this a habit. Once you master it, it will serve you well. She will be in charge. Women like to be in charge and us men have to let them think they are in charge," he said. "She will be in your bed cuddling tonight and every night!"

Janice had endured the funeral and it was televised on all the local channels. She was not going to let them see her face. She wore a black veil over her face, and sat with his parents.

The cemetery was full of officers from all over the state, and even some from throughout all the states across America. They came to honor the fallen officer and give him due respect.

Adam stood in the very back of the crowd, out of sight of them until she walked to the car. Before she got in, he stepped onto the pavement, so she could see him. She did, he knew because she stopped for a moment to stare at him. Then she got into the black limousine.

He took the third shift maintenance position. He had always been able to fix most anything that broke. He thought this was the job that he would not have to look at the beautiful woman that was in his head.

Four weeks later he saw his mistake when she walked up to him and said, “I didn’t know you worked here, too?”

“Yeah and I thought you worked in the office during the daytime.” She was in jeans and a sweatshirt, and she looked damn hot. Down boy, he told himself, but she had already seen his response to her. It did not embarrass him, but it was drawing eyes, and he placed the tool box strategically to cover any embarrassment for her.

“Well I got to get dressed. I’ll see you later!” and she walked away. He frowned.

He asked where she worked, hoping not in maintenance. If so, he was going to be in a heap of trouble. He had promised no trouble to Marcus and Auntie, but he would nail her, if she worked in maintenance.

“In security at night and in the office in the day,” she smiled.

He be damned, if she wasn't flirting with him. Or was it his imagination? No she would not give that information to just anyone, so he had some hope.

"I hope I don't get electrocuted thinking about those pair of jeans. Concentrate on your job. Stay clear for the time being." Yes, he was lost into her from the start. She would only want him, if he was a good person. She had a good officer. She will always compare us. "It will never work! It will never work!" he said to himself.

"What will never work?" his boss said.

"I was talking about something that I was going to fix, but I know exactly what will work, and I will fix it. That's one thing boss you can count on me to make it work. I never give up," he said.

"It's just a light socket. It's not rocket science. You weren't talking about that were you son?" the foreman said.

"Truthfully I wasn't," and he continued his job.

"Well ... if you need anything the man upstairs, said to ask?" the boss said.

"No, I'm good, but thanks!" and the boss went on and left him to his agony. She was ingrained in his thought process. Shaking his head, "Those jeans are worth the agony."

PART SEVENTEEN

CHAPTER ONE

Guy and Tate completed their investigation of Vincent Bogart and presented the folder to Mrs. Bogart. He was having an affair with his secretary Clarice, and they had the evidence that Mrs Bogart had requested. She smiled and thanked them and said, “I’ll have you a check in the mail tomorrow. I’ll keep your phone number on speed dial, and tell ALL my friends to ask for your service, if they should need the best P.I. in the business!”

“That is as good as doubling or tripling OUR business! Tate, you will not regret this. GM will be relieved that she gets to stay home,” Guy told him.

“Do you really believe that?” Tate asked with a smirk.

“Nah, I just like saying it! She would turn me over her knee if she heard me.” He was saying it as she entered the office.

“Heard you say what, GS?” Madeline slapped a kiss on the back of his neck and waited. He was quiet as a mouse and went straight to his computer.

She stood in the doorway looking at Tate, “Say what Tate?”

He gulped and said, “Say that we would began to be late for supper now that we have all this business!”

"Good try. Guy will get you in a lot of trouble, if you start lying for him," she looked from one to the other.

"It was a test, Tate. She has very good ears, but her knees are bony!" uy said. She threaten him pointing to the paddle that hung on the wall. THE ONE, she used on him as a little boy.

"It will never happen again. I promise," Tate said standing there with his mouth open. GS was laughing as was GM.

"How was your day dear?" Beatrice sat at the long table smiling and feeding their twin girls, and the twin boys were feeding themselves and fighting using their spoons as swords.

"Pretty good, my dear. Looks like the children are having a scrumptious dinner. What is it?"

"It's Mr Mac Hamburglar, dear. You fry hamburger and throw macaroni and cheese into one pan. They love it and yes Mrs B has the night off as does the new nanny Mrs April."

She continued, "It's you and me buddy," and she grinned and pursed for her kiss. There was nowhere to kiss that did not have food on it. So he blew her an air kiss which she caught and patted her right breast, then her left breast, and he immediately went to wash his hands.

"Amazing how she does that I feel like I just kissed the twin peaks," he was thinking. "Oh Snap! I forgot to kiss the children. She can make me lose all my senses, always has."

"Are you talking to me dear?" she loved to hear him mumble about her breasts.

"Not tonight dear I am busy!" she was giggling so hard that the girls got the giggles.

Roscoe sat at the head of the table and said, "Boys we must be good tonight and do what mommy says so she won't whoop up on your daddy!" and they just howled. "Mommy's going to whoop daddy! Mommy's going to whoop daddy!"

She said, "And I can hardly wait as she stared into his eyes.

He returned her stare without breaking the trance, he said.

"I think I will just have ice creammmm! Sorry I had, too!"

As the night shift was dragging along and a few repairs because the joint is brand new. Adam sat watching a pretty blonde make her rounds, and he made sure his toolbox was in place encase she stopped and spoke. She didn't and he sighed. He took his tool belt off to go get something to eat, and sat at a back table. He was use to eating and doing most everything in the shadows. He watched her order coffee and damn, she was walking toward him. F—! He sipped his coffee.

She said, "Is this chair taken?" clearly it was not. She paused waiting for him to say something.

"No take a load off!" he was berating himself for such a remark and turned his head as if looking for someone.

"Looking for someone?" he finally looked at her for the first time since she sat down. She had the most beautiful eyes and mouth, and tits and stop you fool. He looked away.

"Are you okay?" she asked . "Have I got something on my face or what?"

"No you look like someone I use to know. You didn't go to Wesley High, did you?" good covering up. He told himself.

"No! I went to Jackson High, but I wish I had," Janice said.

Oh hell no, was she saying she wished she had gone because of him. Don't be a fool? and he asked "WHY?"

She was pinching on his cake and devouring it, and licking her fingers. "Mercy!" he said.

"What? I was in a private school and I hated it. Would have loved to run wild like the other kids my age, but had the strictest parents." Janice was killing him with the cake. He pushed the plate to her.

"No, I am on a diet! Just one more finger full, please! Then keep it way over there." She licked her finger and licked it, and he was so hot. He loosened the tie that they made him wear, and swallowed hard.

She knew she was being bad, but he was so handsome and it had been so long. She was sexually starving. He wants me, but he is being polite. I am making an ass out of myself. She stood and he could see her tits were hard, and he stood just so she could see how hard he was. Even in the dark back lighting, she could see he had exactly what she needed. This same person was devouring her with his eyes, and it was drawing her in … big time.

"Gotta go back to work," and she walked away to the nearest restroom. She washed her face and took a wet paper towel, and wipe her neck, and between her breast. She was so hot. She took her phone out and told her boss that she was sick. Then walked to her locker and got her jeans and blouse, and dressed quickly.

As she came out, he was standing there. "Are you okay? I didn't frighten you, if I did I am so sorry!" and he meant it.

She could see he was concerned so she needed to be frank.

"You did nothing. I was asking for it and you delivered. I have not been myself of late. It is just hormones or something. Think nothing of it … BUT... I can never have coffee with you. This is where I work and they will fire me."

"If I touch you, I will be fired." He did not walk near her because the cameras were on, and he had a guard that kept following him as if he didn't know.

He had his back to her, "I want you bad ... but it has to be your move. I will stay away until you come to me. You know my room number," and he walked away.

She was trembling and she could not and would not go to his room. Thank goodness there were cameras, if not I would be there and he would be loving me right now, and doing what I want right now. Over and over it played in her brain. She doubled over, and she saw herself falling to the floor.

She was mentally exhausted. The other security guard had gotten the ammonia, and took her to the break room.

"Honey are you okay?" one of the female officers asked.

"What happened?" "You fainted." "Honey you're not PG?"

"Not that I know of!" she said.

What if I am … it will be Justin's! Then she started crying. No one could stop her or console her.

He was watching the whole thing and wanted to hold her, but could not. She will come to me eventually. He had not heard the part about she could be pregnant.

She went to the doctor the next day, and she was indeed pregnant. She was both happy and sad. This changed everything. She would go back to work tonight and have sex with him. He will think it is his, just the thought of raising a baby by herself was nonexistent. She had to do what she had to do. She was not proud of what she was about to do, but in this hick town, she would never survive alone.

She decided not to work just walk up to him and tell him, "Let's get it on."

Which by grace he was off tonight and having a drink at the bar. She had on a one-piece silver slinky jumpsuit that was strapless and heels. He saw her walk in and he almost spilled his drink. She was walking straight to his table.

She motioned for him to follow, and he was about to break a leg getting around the table. Her long flowing blonde curls were bouncing as she walked in those heels, and her buttocks were swaying in the slinky outfit. What in the hell am I going to do? She is walking to my frigging room.

"Open it!" she said leaning in to kiss his cheek nothing else.

"Yes Ma'am! Are you sure? I can back off here, but I may not be able to when we get inside."

"Open the door! If you want me before I change my mind!"

He opened it and she walked to the bed, and waited as he put on the inside lock on the door, and bolted the world out.

He kicked his boots off and turned her to him. She kicked off her shoes and they were the same height. She had not looked up, but placed her hands on his chest and rubbed all his muscles. Then unbuttoned his shirt one by one, pulled the shirttail out, and began unbuckling, and he stopped her. He kissed her gently. He had been too long without a woman so he wanted her fully ready for him before he took his pants off.

She was kissing him with need, and her tits were hard and rubbing across his chest. She had no bra or panties on, so when she unzipped the side of her jumpsuit, it fell to the floor. She was completely naked.

The lamp was on and he feasted his eyes on the most beautiful breasts, flat stomach, clean shaven. "Oh I can't stop Janice! I can't! You are everything I have ever wanted. Why me?"

And she touched him and rubbed him. "Does it really matter?"

"Not really. It seems you have made up your mind way before we got here, and I am not going to disappoint you. I promise," he found her vaginal button and circled it till she was panting with need.

"Please don't make me beg!" she said.

He took his pants off, but not his briefs. He thought she needed to see how large he was, and see if she thought she could take all of it or half of it, while he had one grain of sense left. This he needed to know. So he asked, "Do you want all or half of me?"

She had her arms around him and grinding on his briefs and said, "I want all you can give me and I want it all night long."

He was breathing heavy in her ear, "I Gotta! So please lay down. I might drop us."

She lay down situated it ... a little at a time . . . expanding with each tiny movement.

"Oh! Adam Adam ADAM!" and they fulfilled all of their longings. She was grabbing his shoulders and licking his ear, and he was kissing on her breast until the explosion like neither had ever had happened. Wave after wave followed and it was like they could not get enough of each other.

"OH baby ... you are squeezing me so tight and I am going to take another ride, if you will let me? Help me," he said and she raised her hips up further to met him.

"Oh Adam! Why is it so good? I have never had it this good in my entire life! I knew it! You knew it!" she gasped.

"You know you are mine now. No one will ever touch you but me. You have too say it. WILL YOU marry me?" he was still inside holding what she wanted and wanted so badly. "Say it."

"I will marry you, if you promise to do this every chance we get, day or night and anytime in between," Janice begged.

He was beginning to move and he let her on top and said,

"I want you until neither of us can breathe," and they did until they fell asleep intertwined. Throughout the night, they coupled and hung on for dear life.

She had no idea what his past was, and HE prayed she would not reject him when she found out.

SHE prayed, he would not reject her when he found out that she was pregnant with her dead fiancee's baby.

Neither had to work until the night shift the following day.

They dressed and went for a marriage license and got married by the Justice of the Peace. Then went to work that night smiling, and boy were they smiling.

They did their jobs and met in his room to slake their unmet desires of this day. Every day would be a new set of desires some more insatiable than others, but still intense for both.

He had to tell his Aunt Eunice and Marcus, and have them meet his new bride.

He was working so hard to make a future for them. She was just so happy. Every time someone met her, she was smiling.

Auntie Eunice fell in love with her as did Ellen.

Marcus said he could judge that this boy was going to be alright. "No need for you two to live in a hotel. You are family and must stay with us."

Marcus said, "You tell them my wife."

Eunice said, "Adam we have twenty bedrooms in our house. Corey and Ellen live with us, and of course Jason. So it will be no imposition. That's seventeen to pick from!"

Eunice was so excited that she hugged Janice, and Marcus hugged Adam.

"It is your call Janice. Where do you want to live?" Adam asked looking at her to make a choice for them.

"Your aunt and uncle have made me very welcome. I think it's a no brainer. With them unless, you don't want to?"

Walking to her car she asked, "Why are you a maintenance man and your family is rich?" "I'll tell you one day!" he said.

CHAPTER TWO

Tate got a call from Adam that he was married and he wanted Debbie to meet his Janice.

Tate was hollering and it brought the whole house to the living room running. They thought he was hurt.

"Tate, guess what else? Auntie wants us to live with them," Adam was crying. Janice had no clue why, and kissed him.

"I told you if you worked hard, good things would come your way from these wonderful people. I am so proud of you, and yes we will all meet her. I'll let the women set it up."

They agreed to the weekend when the newlyweds were off.

Madeline said, "Okay Tate give?"

"Adam got married and wants us to meet her, and they are living at Aunt Eunice's. He has proved himself like I knew he would," Tate was hugging Madeline, then Trevor, and lastly kissing his Debbie.

Janice had her arm around Adam and he said, "MY little brother is a wise man, and you are the woman that has saved my life Janice. I love you honey. When we get situated, I am going to buy you a huge ring," Adam said.

Janice said, "I don't need rings and things. All I need is you! I am not a fancy person. I have worked hard. Two jobs to pay for a little apartment. OH MY … I have to get my stuff out before the first of the month."

"Don't fret you two. I'll have a moving van go by or we can give what you don't need to charity. Once you pick out your room, you can make those decisions. How about we go to THE INN and celebrate?" Marcus said and held Eunice's hand.

Jason was so happy that Charlie came with them to dinner. All the grownups were talking. So they were playing their action games at the table which was good in a way, but Corey said, "Dude you got to slack up on those games."

"It is summertime Corey! Don't worry when school starts, I will. You are gone to work all the time, and the grownups do their thing, and all I got is my games. I can play with my friends on XBOX like they are sitting beside me in my room. So what's the harm?" Jason asked.

"Okay be warned you should be reading classic novels by now, so when you get to high school you will have them down pat." Corey was playing father. He had done it for the last eight years. It was hard to break the habit of caring for his little brother. He had to back off now that Marcus has come into the picture.

He didn't know this Charlie kid, and something didn't feel right. He knew first hand how sneaky some of the teenagers were today. He has been sticking like glue to Jason. He was going to ask Ellen to spy on them when he was at work. The summer is a good time for mischief. "Dang! I must be growing up. I'm talking like my mother. Ha ha! … yuck!"

Jennifer was the nerd, Jason thought and now Corey thinks he is a brain. No one has thought about how much I miss Coraine. "I don't know what happened, but I cried and no one would talk to me, I was too little. Well I'm not little any more. I have been on the internet and looked up the drugs, she had. Never do drugs, but want to know why? I need to understand," Jason said to himself

Charlie knew everything about drugs. He knew the names, what it would do to you.

Jason asked, "How you know all this?"

"Cause I try them for fun!" Charlie said. "I like getting high. You aught to try it sometime, just for fun! You need a little fun this summer!"

Ellen said, "Why that little punk" … Corey is going to kill Mr Charlie unless I talk to someone. If I don't before ADAM gets here, they may say any drugs found in the house are his. She marched herself to Marcus because Eunice would never understand.

"Mr Marcus can I talk to you in private. It is REAL important," she couldn't stand still.

"Come into my office," he walked to the desk and ask Ellen to sit in Adriana's chair that was called the hot seat.

"Corey has been suspecting that this Charlie was up to no good, so he asked me to spy on him and Jason. This boy has drugs on him and is offering them to Jason. He said no, but Charlie is saying how much FUN he can have this summer if he tries them. Corey will freak out. Your wife will freak out and poor Adam can't be around them, or he will go back to jail. You do know about Coraine and her death?" Ellen finally had it all out.

Marcus was absorbing all this information and he told her he did not know, and that Eunice had not told him. "She said she would in time."

"She committed suicide on drugs. It nearly destroyed my Corey and mother Eunice. She never really recovered because she won't talk about it! Please don't let that boy back in this house, please!" Ellen was pleading. She was afraid Corey would kill him with his bare hands.

"Now dear, you don't worry I will get to the bottom of this," Marcus patted her on the back and hugged her.

"If you heard it, then one of my guards heard it, too! We will have a little powwow and fix this situation. You are a brave girl. Now relax. I will speak to Jason and Corey together. I may need to take Eunice to the doctor afterward. Will you go sit with her, if I get busy!" Marcus asked.

"Of course I will do anything!" Ellen didn't know if she could keep quiet, but she was going to try.

Marcus called a meeting with his guards. "Which one of you has been monitoring Jason?"

They all said they had from time to time.

"So why was it not reported to me that Jason's little friend Charlie has been bringing drugs into this house and trying to get Jason to try them?" he was furious and Eunice heard him, and she sat down outside of the room and listened.

"This CANNOT and will not be tolerated in this household!"

Marcus asked, "Is that clear gentlemen?"

One said, "This is the norm for most affluent homes these days, sir. I do apologize and it will be handled posthaste."

"It better be and the place searched. This boy nor his parents are never to step on this property. Wherever Jason goes, he is to be protected from this kind of behavior. Is that clear?" Marcus wanted to repeat it so it was good and clear.

"Yes, sir," in unison and they left his office.

"Come out Eunice and talk to me," Eunice came in and sat down wringing her hands.

"We are going to have to have a talk with Jason this afternoon. Do you want me to talk with him or do you want US to talk to him?" he asked.

"I think we together should talk to him. I need to know what to say to him. I just don't know anything about drugs? I didn't even know my Coraine was using drugs until she was dead, and I blamed myself for not seeing it," Eunice had her head bowed. He went and hugged her.

"Ellen is terrified that Corey will get into trouble. So I think Corey needs to be in our family meeting. What do you think? And we will ALL go to classes as a family and learn about what to look for. Eunice, I had no idea either. We must inform Adam and Janice when they move in. I need to call Trevor and see if he has some information on this Charlie family," Marcus was thinking out loud and trying to cover all the bases.

"Roscoe will know the family because he knows everyone in town. He was a police officer for years before he went into security. Charlie is such a nice talking young boy. I'm shocked. Jason is in for a surprise tonight," she said.

"Adriana darling, how are you feeling? I have a family situation and need your expert advice. Do you feel up to it?"

Marcus never stammered so his daughter was worried.

"Daddy sit down and take a breath. The answer to the first question is, I am fine and bored. Second question, of course. Fire away!" Adriana looked at Unitus.

Marcus filled her in. She winked at Unitus.

"I think I can call and have the bastard arrested before supper and in juvie by morning,'" Adriana sighed.

"Be serious daughter … this is not funny," Marcus was unnerved to say the least.

"Daddy you handle billion dollar deals and you can't handle a twelve year old? You handled me. I take that back, it was the nanny when I brought that weed in one time."

Unitus was freaking out … pointing to her.

"I was nine, Unitus. Nine!" she told him while listening to her father and covering the phone.

"Daddy you'll do fine. Jason probably doesn't even know he's been played by this Charlie, and it can be a lesson well learned. Of course, the nanny tore my tail up. Legally I can have you arrested for child abuse, so don't do that and that's my advice. Yes I can get you the class scheduled, and I'll sign you all up myself. Yes, I will kiss him for you and take a picture. Bye enough!" Adriana hung up.

"Now where were we? She bared her breast and Unitus made a sucking sound. She said, "For Real? Hand me my boy! Now!" Unitus was squeezing her tit and Vanderbilt was chomping down.

"That's my boy. I just wanted to help him darling!"

"No! Unitus. I know I have two, but you want it all and poor baby would have none," Adriana was shaking her head.

"Okay I had to try it... that was the most fun I'll have for six weeks! Watching my son savor my wife's beautiful huge breasts. Okay I am going into the bathroom and sit, I can't watch. Let me know when he is through," he said.

"Whatcha doing in there? You're too quiet," she asked.

"Wouldn't you like to know?" he said.

"I'm coming in, if you don't tell me," she threatened.

"Well I have to fart! So don't push that red button,"

"Oh I won't dare because they would call in the SWAT team to defuse that bomb!" she said.

He comes out and says, "You are the only woman that has to know what her husband is doing at all times."

"NO, I do not. I'm the only woman that let's her husband suck the milk out of her breast because it feels damn good … and then he doesn't understand why his stomach is upset!"

Due to the shouting in the room, the nurses had gathered in the hallway and the older nurse said, "You' all think these two are fighting, don't you? Well think again, It's foreplay. They may start having sex any minute like they did last time!"

They all ran to the charting room as fast as they could run.

"I knew I could give you some privacy" talking to the wall.

Unitus said, "Thanks!"

"You're welcome!" the nurse said marching to the chart room.

Corey brought Jason in by the nape of his shirt and sat him down, Ellen had told him. They all were looking at Jason.

"What's wrong? What' d I do?" he really had no clue.

Marcus started, "You may or may not have done anything wrong. We don't know, but your friend has. Hasn't he? and he then knew exactly what they were talking about. Did you know he was bringing drugs into my house young man?"

"Yes, sir! But he promised me, he wouldn't do them while he was here and he didn't I swear. He said he did them at his house. He wanted me to try, but I said NO. I wanted to know about them because of Coraine. Everyone said I was too little to know about them. Well I am not little any more, but no one will talk about it now either."

"I am proud of you for not trying them. I commend you for that. Did you know that the parents get held accountable, if drugs are found in their home and can have to go to court?"

His eyes dilated, "No sir I did not. I would never have let him in, if I had known that."

"I believe you son, and this is a learning experience for all of us! So you say you want to learn! Then we will all go to classes this summer and learn the laws and learn what to look out for. You will be getting older and if you get in a car and it has drugs in it. You go to jail, too. I don't want to see that happen to you nor do I want your mother distressed over it. You have to say no, not only to drugs, but you have to say no to people who have drugs on them. Pick your friends wisely. Your friends that are drug-free are always welcome here."

"I will. I promise. Thank you for getting me classes so I can learn and so mom can learn, too! I am sorry mama about Charlie. He is the only friend I have had since we moved here. I use to have you Corey, but you are married now and that is okay. Mr. Marcus you are the best thing that has happened to our family. You are like a father to me and I am sorry that I let you down."

Corey said, "Anytime you need answers I am here for you, I feel I let you down Jason. I am sorry," and he hugged his little brother.

Eunice said, "I am so glad this is cleared up before Adam and Janice moved in. Marcus my gratitude is two-fold. Ellen you did a good thing. Come and let me give you a hug." She came and hugged her tightly. Corey hugged Jason.

"Jason this has been a learning experience for both of us. You and I neither know anything about drugs. If I had known these things before, your sister would probably not be dead."

"That's not true Eunice. You cannot hold yourself to blame for what those seven boys did. They were to blame, not you!So don't ever say that again in this house. You have been a good mother. Now you are a good wife. This family will be thankful that Charlie and his kind will never be welcome here. Does anyone else want to say anything?"

No one did and they all went to their rooms.

CHAPTER THREE

Madeline was in her swimming suit and modest cover-up, and Trevor in his safari short outfit, and they were headed for the unveiling of THE BOAT. Down at the boathouse, they walked through and went to the lakeside deck. She turned to him and said, “Happy Birthday, honey!”

He kissed her and bent her backwards in a dip. “Remind me to take you dancing darling, and thank you for the boat. I do think we ought to name it, and have a christening party after we break it in.” He winked and helped her on board.

“A name for her. Hmm … You do the honors,” she sat on the deck’s chaise and patted the seat beside her.

“GM & TP’s Love Nest,” Trevor said and grinned.

“You can’t be serious. The grand kids would want to know what a love nest is?” Madeline grabbed his hand.

“Lazy Days?” Trevor questioned.

“What about Floating Southfork?” Madeline said as if a light bulb went off.

“Or Floating & Fishing?” he had got them a bottle of lemonade out of the fridge.

“You’ll be floating and I’ll be fishing,” said Trevor as he poured them a glass.

"I actually like that," she said and sipped the cool beverage.

"You want to go below and get your OTHER birthday present?" she winked and started for the stairs.

Tate and Debbie had gone on the motorcycle to THE HOTEL to meet Janice and Adam. Corey and Ellen had also took their bike to meet them.

"We have come to help with the move," Tate said.

"Follow me!" Adam had rented a U-Haul so Janice could take her time and move only what she wanted. Far less after she saw the mansion, and their bedroom was as big as her whole tiny apartment.

"We decided not to trash the palace with my shabby furni-ture and I will just box the personal stuff up that I cherish," Janice said.

When they walked in Adam said, "This a nice place Janice. You can take anything you want to, Babe." He saw a police uniform in a photo and knew it was Justin.

He picked it up and stared at the man in the picture. Janice took it from him and said, "I am packing it away. That is my past. You are my future and I love you," she wrapped her arms around his neck, and he held her so tight.

"We have a future that many do not have and I don't want either of us to look BACKWARDS," and he kissed her gently on the lips.

Corey and Tate were staring, "Ahem! Ahem! Sorry, but our wives are jealous! Keep it up and the landlord might make you move because of the orgy up here," and they all started kissing their spouses and laughing.

They pitched in and got it all done and there was nothing left that she wanted, and left it for Goodwill to pick up. They jumped in the van, and the bikes followed them to the mansion. They unloaded everything into the newlyweds' bedroom with Aunt Eunice pointing out the pull down ladder. It was stairs to the attic where there was extra storage space.

"Thanks that is a good place to put pictures and luggage and things we won't use every day," Janice said.

They were all tired and hungry when in walks Marcus, "You' all about finished? Because I ordered us a feast and it is in the big dinner hall. Just ready to chow down myself," and he smiled at Eunice who was hugging Jason.

They all sat and talked about the move and laughed about the pretend orgy which raised Eunice's eyebrows, and a chuckle from Marcus. He had blessed the table and was happy he had more children to love.

His children were scattered everywhere, and they never called unless they wanted something. "No news is good news, he told himself. He would call Adriana later, she was the only one that never asked for anything. She always preferred to work for it. She even put herself through lawyer school.

"This is my family now and I love you all. Eunice has made me a happy man. I want you all to feel welcome and I am a good listener. If anyone needs me, I am here for you! Drive home safely, and we older ones will retire for the night!" and he and Eunice went laughing as they walked down the hall to their bedroom.

The young couple had picked a room further away from everyone. Corey and Ellen's bedroom was in the middle of the mansion. Jason's was on the top floor near Eunice, but not so near that he crowded them.

He was happy to have his privacy especially after the ordeal with Charlie. He had his own video game room, and the theater room was up there. As well as the room with the pool table and Foosball table, another of Jason's favorites.

Janice and Adam were exhausted. When Adam got in the marble shower with five jets and was all lathered up, Janice eased in with him. She asked, "Need any help?"

Everything came back to life, and they savor the love-making, they had suppressed all day. It was worth the wait.

Now that this was their first home as a married couple, they wanted the first night to be spectacular. With the jets pulsating she didn't think it would ever stop. She told him, "We might just break the world's record, you know!"

"I know and it is too wonderful. Some people are married to the wrong people, and I know without a shadow of a doubt that you were made for me and only me!" Adam was tearful.

"I needed to tote you over the threshold, but I forgot. So I'll tote you to bed. We can pretend this bathroom doorjamb is the front door, okay?" she nodded.

He tried to lay her down, but she stood in the middle of the bed. "I want you to remember this night forever, so lie down husband." He grinned in anticipation. He laid on his stomach.

"No way cowboy. Roll over and take your medicine."

"Do you think you can handle it?" Adam asked.

Janice was moaning so loud, as they climaxed.

Then they slept. He woke and lay staring at her and the room, and still could not believe this was real. His ache was evident that this woman was his equal. He had said he had no equal, and she had proven him wrong. She had proven to him that she loved him. Each day their lovemaking got bolder and bolder. He could hardly wait for tomorrow ... to experiment with her … was heaven.

The family met on Sunday afternoon to greet Adriana and Unitus home with their little bundle of joy. Angel was with Debbie and Tate at the boathouse.

When she saw her daddy toting her mommy and a little baby blanket, she ran to them. Unitus sat down on one of the rockers on the porch, and Angel climbed up.

"Let me see. Let me see daddy. Brodder! My Brodder!. Unitus picked them all up, and Tate held the door.

"Man you are strong. How much do you lift when you work out?" Tate was impressed.

Adriana said, "500 lbs and he says I am a featherweight. Isn't that something?" She loved bragging on her man.

The baby was on her shoulder and Unitus was tickling Angel so she got down.

"Daddy stop. Mommy make Daddy stop!" Angel begged.

"It tickles! Okay Daddy you can do it again!" She just wanted attention. Adriana handed Unitus, little Vanderbilt and played with Angel.

"Mommy missed her Angel. Did you have fun with Daddy while Mommy was gone?" then Angel rattle off a stream of things that they had done.

"WOW I hated I missed that!" she had her mommy's attention. Now she was moving on to Grandpa Marcus.

Everyone gathered to see their new little boy and Adriana had had a onesie made for him that read, "The next MR. UNIVERSE."

Unitus was beaming, "That's my boy!"

The family had gathered for a cookout and a christening of the boat. The celebration was also for the new family member and he had a cake, "Welcome home Mark Van Pommel."

Madeline thanked all for coming and they announced the name of their Boat which was a small yacht ... "Floating & Fishing."

A toast from Trevor and all raised their glasses, "I am a grateful man to have such a good family and extraordinary good friends. From this day forward the women can float and we men can fish ... all we want. Since the women have to know where we all are at all times, instead of them telephoning us and scaring the fish off ... I have purchased each a pair of high powered binoculars. Please WOMEN pick them up and make a check by your name. I am expecting to hear flax from this. Beside the glasses are a set of high powered earplugs, please MEN take a set and check your name off. Feel free to use either ASAP. Let's eat!"

"Here! Here!" and they made their way to the long buffet table of Shrimp and Lobster, Baked Potatoes and Corn on the Cob with fresh baked Cornbread. The coffee urn was set up as was the Lemonade and Iced Tea fountains. It was going to be followed by Strawberry Shortcake and barn dancing. The stereo was already getting pumped up to the max volume.

Everyone was happy except the new Mark, he was hungry. Unitus whispered to Trevor, and he picked up Adriana. She asked Debbie to watch Angel. Janice said, "I'd would love to, if you don't mind?"

Janice needed to learn how and today looked like a good start. Adam was watching her and smiling.

Debbie said, "We can do it together. No problem Adriana."

Adriana whispered in her ear that she was going to breast-feed the baby and change him.

Unitus was still holding Adriana and the baby, and he walked to the back door. Then onto the boat, and down the steps to the cabin with the double bed. He laid them down, then propped her up. "Do you need your pain medicine?" she nodded yes.

"I' ll be right back," Unitus said. He stood their watching the miracle happen. The boy had already latched on to her right breast and was making Adriana squirm.

He wanted to leap over the fence, but this artificial leg wouldn't let him . He needed his blade leg. Mumbling to himself because it was going to take longer to go through the boathouse, and back with Adriana in so much pain.

Little Vanderbilt was being burped, and he had grabbed the diaper bag. While Adriana was taking her medicine, he did the fatherly duty. He changed his diaper, and burped him.

"I am so glad to have you home honey! Now just lie down and rest. I'll put him on the other side when he is asleep, and you 'all can take a snooze. Here is your phone, call me if you need me okay?"

She would rest better, and he was going back in. So he could care for Angel, then he saw she had plenty babysitters.

So he walked to where the men had gathered at the bar.

He was asked what kind of drink did he want the bartender to make him?

"No, can't drink. I'm on DADDY DUTY," and he smiled.

CHAPTER FOUR

Beatrice was so proud of the twins, BeBe and FiFi were potty trained. Now all were diaper free, it was a lighter load in traveling. Kyleigh and she had plans to go to Carowinds, and spend the day. They didn't have to take the strollers any more.

Their new system was everyone holds hands and one mother in the front and one mother in the back.

The nanny, Mrs A and the housekeeper Mrs B were asked if they wanted to come along? They both said quickly, "No you all go and have a good day, ladies!"

BeBe and FiFi were destined to be clothes hounds when they grew up. The grandmother Inga was forever bringing over cute little dresses that she had designed for them. Today they were wearing a pink flowery ruffled A-line dress and pink tennis shoes.

Before Roscoe left for work, they had to model them for him and of course, Beatrice had instructed them how. "You like daddy?" "Mommy?" Mother and father were grinning .

They were jumping up and down about the theme park.

"Roscoe we have to have a talk," Beatrice said.

His eyes opened wider and he asked with concern, "Okay anytime, any day, anywhere!" he stated and looked into her eyes and grinned wider.

"Honey you have such a one tracked mind, bring them eyes back up here." He had focused on her breasts.

She snapped her fingers, "Up here! We have to decide our triplets names. Do think about it seriously. No weird names, please!" his eyes went from her breasts to her face.

He kissed her, "Now why would you say that?"

"I already have been thinking Elijah call him Eli, Ezra and Elvis. Always wanted me an Elvis. If there is a girl, Elisa or Eloise. How about that?"

"Elvis, really? But you have been thinking in the E list of names, I see." Beatrice said with a smile.

She added, "I went to the J's like Johnny, Jessy and Jerry. If we have girls we can change the Y to IE and it works?"

"So you went to the J list. Hmm we will talk about it later. Have fun and if you 'all need help, just call GUY!" he smiled.

"Just joking! Take pictures. Text them to me!" then Roscoe kissed Beatrice passionately and went to work.

Beatrice loaded up and they stopped by to pick up Kyleigh and Madison.

Off they went to the amusement park, and all the kids were screaming as they pulled in. "I want to ride. I don't wanna. I like clowns. Where are the clowns? Animals? Mommy?"

They all wanted different things. The four year olds were all inquisitive. The three year olds were quick on their feet, and these two girls were going to be their focus for sure.

"What were we thinking Beatrice?" Kyleigh said.

"This is a good day! I may have to rest often. These triplets are already becoming burdensome. I have to pee every five minutes, so be warned. We can get some park strollers, if we have to. We will just take it an hour or maybe two, and we'll get back to sanity. Okay?" Beatrice said and smiled at her best friend.

"Whatever you say! I am good with it. Let's get them to lock their hands and play train!" Kyleigh laughed. She had done this many times with first graders, but never with this age. She missed teaching but Madison and Guy were her only priorities now.

Some bozo said, "It looks like the zoo came to town, and look Margaret she is having some more."

His wife poked him and said, "Shut up Harold before I whack you one for real!" She told the girls, "Sorry!"

"No problem ma'am, we hear that from GENTLEMEN every day!" and Beatrice stared with beady eyes at Harold.

"The Moron!" Kyleigh said. They went onto the kiddie athletic equipment where they climbed, and jumped, and ran in circles till they were worn out. They got some carts and only two could they push.

So Be Be and Fi Fi got in one of the Park's double strollers and Madison could jump on back or push them. Beatrice had the other double stroller, Cain and Caleb loved to ride.

They had all the pictures they needed, and they would stop my McDonald's and get them Happy Meals, and zoom home.

The women smiled and said how much they were enjoying this. Beatrice said, "You know next year, I will have a zoo for sure, and we will have to bring the men along. Darn it!"

Kyleigh said,"Yeah, don't want them to miss out on FUN!"

Bruce and Jana had walked up the mountain to check on the new parents. Little Vanderbilt was in his blue room.

"He was up all night. Now Vanderbilt is sleeping. Please wake him so we might sleep tonight!" Adriana said laughing, and grabbed a pillow to hold tight.

"It still hurts to laugh or cough and I forget." The men had gone for the baby. Adriana showed Jana her stomach sutures.

"Yeah this pregnancy is going to take me longer to recover. Unitus and I are talking about him working six months, and then I work six months. So we both can have quality time with the kids," Adriana was grimacing because she had never been the stay at home kind of wife.

Angel came running and jumped in Jana's lap.

"Anytime you need a break … just call me or Debbie. Even if it is just so you can take a nap," Jana added.

"A nap! Now you are talking my language. Thank you I will, if Unitus goes to work. I have a back log of cases, and he can fill in for me, and we can talk about them at night. It will give me that outlet, so my brain doesn't completely shutdown while on maternity leave," Adriana said.

"Unitus, darling can I hold him." Jana got up and Unitus had to pat her on the head and measure her. She swatted him.

"Somethings never change like your height and our friendship. I love you two!" he said while Bruce held Angel and smiled at his wife.

"Same here. Good friendships are hard to find these days!"

"Here!Here!" they woke the baby. "Uh Oh, you're in trouble!"

The man in the shadows was watching Adam working on an elevator light bulb replacement. He was one of Adam's old roommates in prison.

"He thinks he is going to screw over me, and get by with it. I'll show him!" Lonnie was talking to himself. Lonnie didn't know that Adam's bodyguard was watching him and so was Janice.

Janice had been a police woman before working in security, and she had remembered this man's face from a mugshot. His face was distinctive. A scar on his left cheek in the shape of a half moon, and a tattoo of a bull under it. He was a Mexican drug dealer then. He sold drugs or transported them, and which was he doing now? That was the big question.

She knew he was up to no good. She was watching him and told her fellow guard to watch him, also.

He walked up to Adam. Adam froze, looking him squarely in the eye. "Long time, no see!"

"Get out of here! If you know what is good for you!"

"And just what you gonna do about it whimp, if I don't?"

Lonnie sneered and walked into the elevator. Adam stared at the closed door.

If this man was here. There was a job fixing to go down. He would not be able to afford a room in this hotel unless someone was funding him. When transporting they usually drove straight through to their delivery destination, it was something else and he needed to find out. If he did make a scene and was involve in any way, Adam knew he would go back to prison and lose everything.

Adam was terrified for his wife also, if something went down she would be in the middle of it. That was her job. He had to see her, and make sure she steered clear of this man. He could not bear the thought of her being harmed.

Lonnie had seen Adam kiss this woman in the parking lot.

She maybe a good hostage, if this robbery didn't go as planned. Knowing Adam, he'd kill for this piece of ass! Lonnie told himself, just play it cool. He laughed and said, "this is payback time," as he opened the door to his room.

There sat his accomplices in this heist. THE HOTEL was not their target. It was THE CASINO next door, it had been hopping with business since the grand opening.

People were coming from everywhere to gamble here. The TAKE would be over a million. On Sunday night, it was overflowing with big time gamblers, and the Brinxx truck would come on Monday morning in the wee hours, between five and six o'clock. They would be ready.

The goons he had with him were Rocky the Squirrel who was a little Afro American that had got his name as an amateur prize fighter. He would squirrel his dope up his rectum.

The other unsavory character was called The Iceman. He was Hispanic and he had no feelings for anyone or any thing, except for his heroin. He was cold as ice. He would cut you and watch you bleed, laughing as life left your body. The deal was set and Adam had better not interfere... or else!

PART EIGHTEEN

CHAPTER ONE

"Life is good, and fishing makes it better. What you think Marcus?" Trevor was casting his fishing rod into the middle of the lake.

"I couldn't agree more. This is the life!" Marcus cast his off the opposite side, and they sat and talked.

"You see what I see?" Trevor asked.

"Yep! I'm glad you bought those binoculars. They reflect in the sun. They are spying on us early. No phone a ringing, though. Don't miss that a bit!" Marcus admitted.

"Kinda nice that they miss us, but every now and then a man needs a break," Trevor said.

"Yep and I got a bite! It's a big one. Look at that probably a ten-pounder," Marcus was so exciting.

"Trevor, help! I have never caught a fish," Marcus was reeling it in.

"Just relax and hold it tight! I will get the net and bucket, and show you. Don't panic my friend."

Marcus sat real still and held on. Trevor got the bass in the net, and threw him in the fish locker made in the side of the boat. It had water in it and the fish flipped his tail, and splashed Marcus right in the face.

"That's another first! Got to get a picture of my first catch!"

"Are you saying you have never been fishing?" Trevor was shocked.

"No. Never!" Marcus frowned. "You know the crowd I ran with. The yachts and the planes, and the jet-setters. They didn't want to have slime on their hands. All they ever wanted to do was sunbathe and drink!"

"Yeah, I don't miss that crowd a bit. A bunch of phonies. They have their kind of fun and we have ours. I wish them well!" Trevor said. Then he got a bite.

The two men sat and talked, and fished till all most sun-down. The women had to come down and to see their catch and were surprised. Madeline said, "That's dinner who's cooking?"

"Now darling, these we will save until we catch enough for everyone. Then we can have a big wingding," Trevor said.

"Yes and that means we got to fish at least twice a week to catch that many," Marcus smiled and blew Eunice a kiss.

"Okay Eunice! Now you and I have to learn how to fish!" Madeline said holding her nose as if the fish stink.

"Not me! I am scared of those wiggling things. I'll just watch or read a book. Okay?" Eunice cowered and shivered looking at the fish.

"You will be fine, dear. I can show you," Marcus was really taking the bull by the horns after his first day of fishing. He wanted to teach his wife everything. It would be like he was the great fisherman. Trevor could teach him it all soon.

"Okay if you put it that way, my love," Eunice smiled.

Tate and Corey were really enjoying their bikes and Debbie and Ellen were really enjoying holding onto their husbands.

"We gotta get Adam one of these so they can come with us. Let's swing by and talk to them. No they'll be sleeping after working all night," Ellen said.

Janice and Adam didn't get in till ten this morning.

Janice asked Adam how he knew that guy with the scar face. "I know he was sneering at you and talking. I saw it on my camera."

He didn't answer her at first, but knew she would just keep on. So he said, "Let's get some sleep Janice. Don't worry your pretty little head about that stupid guy."

"No way are you going to sleep without talking to me. I know that guy," Janice said.

He swung around and asked, "What do you mean you know that guy?" Adam was in shock.

"From the police station mugshot, we arrested him before. He is evil to the core, but you know that don't you? So come clean Adam. This is your wife that you are talking to!" Janice was standing over him as he sat on the bed.

"I was in prison with him," there it was. Her mouth flew open. "I told you I was never going to look back ... but you just had to keep on. You can leave me, if you must. I did not lie to you because you never asked. I loved you so much. I thought it would be years before you found out or at least I was hoping to prove to you that my past was just that … my past."

She hugged his head to her chest, "I married you for better or worse. I am going nowhere. You can tell me when you are ready. Just be careful with this man. I don't think I could live without you Adam. I have loved, but I have never loved anyone like I love you. It terrifies me that you could get hurt. I saw the way that man looked at you," Janice stated.

"If I should get in trouble defending myself, I will go back to prison. But if he ever harms you, I will gladly rip him apart. You are the air I breath. He will be watching me and he will see us together. He is planning something big. I just don't know what yet! I need to talk to your boss Roscoe. He needs to know. Let's get some sleep now that you know all that I know. We can sleep, or?"

"Or sounds good to me. Then we will sleep better."

"I agree," kissing her. "So much better!'

When they awoke, Adam got on the phone with Roscoe and told him everything he knew about Lonnie. "If I help get him, will I get in trouble. I have to know because I have so much to lose. You of all people know that. Whatever this man is up to. IT is big time! Either drug smuggling or robbery, that's his MO. Talk later," Adam hung up and hugged Janice.

She said, "I'm pregnant!"

He said, "I knew you would be with the way we have been going at it! Just the touching it with your leg is driving me up the wall. She rubbed her leg up and down and said, "Just one more time. I need you, just one more time today!" before I have to tell you. You are not the father. Adam undid her robe.

Madeline heard from "Raven" she was now Michelle Swanson and living in Cincinnati, Ohio. She gave her full address and telephone number.

Madeline called immediately, "Hi Michelle. How are you doing? I think of you often."

Raven said, "I am so glad someone does. I am doing better. I have enrolled in design school. Something I always wanted to do. How is Mr. Trevor?"

"He's his same old lovable self. We don't change much. I can hardly wait for you to come and see us and meet your family. We told you that you are one of our family now, and we meant it!"

Madeline heard a sigh.

"That is something, I have never had … a family! I can hardly wait to visit. The man said another year, and I should be okay to come and see you."

"Until then stay strong and write when you can and call. Hopefully Trevor will be here to talk next time you call. OUR love goes with you each day in everything you do. We are there in spirit. We believe in you, remember that until next time. Take care." If not for Raven, they ALL would be dead.

"Okay and thank you. I am not use to saying the word yet because it is strange to me. But for what it is worth I am learning through you people that love does exist. Until next time tell Trevor hello for me, and set me a place at the table until I can come there. No goodbyes... See ya!"

That night they set her a place at the table just for her.

Jason had no friends now that Charlie wasn't around. It was summertime and he was in a new neighborhood and no one to even skateboard with. He loved the new house and all the "stuff", but he had to make new friends this fall.

He was talking to some girl on the chatline named Cheri and she said she was thirteen also, but she looked older.

It was nice to have someone to talk to and he could pour his heart out. She was going to a nearby school and was a cheerleader. She sent him pictures of her in her uniform.

"We will be practicing soon, and I will let you know when. Maybe you can come and see me."

They started Skype and could see each other.

"You do want to see me right?" she was pulling on her lower lip, been sucking on her finger. She looked weird like a two year old, and then she blew his mind. She began feeling of herself and he quickly cut it off.

His hormones were kicking in big time. He did not answer her continuous twitter and email attempts. He had to talk to Corey. He had to handle himself or Marcus and his mom would kill him after the Charlie incident.

"OMG she is in my head. She is doing this to get me to do something, I am so not ready for," he told himself.

"Corey we got to talk and talk now. You got to help me!"

"Whoa whoa! What kind of trouble are you in now, little brother? Just talk to me," Corey said into his cell phone.

"Come to my room. It's private stuff. You have to see this!" Jason was beside himself when Corey got there.

"Calm down Jason. If you haven't kill someone, we can work it out," Corey had a way with words. Jason laughed.

"I about killed myself getting the computer to shut down," and he explained about this girl. "I don't know what to do. You got to see this and tell me everything that I need to know and how to do IT!" He was holding himself.

"Are you asking me about sex?" he looked at Jason in a condescending way. "I know you need guidance, but I am not the one to give it. Then again I am the only one you should talk about this with. It would freak Mom out, and Marcus would raise the roof and ground you forevermore," Corey was pacing in Jason's room.

"Do you really want me to see this?" Corey was not happy.

Jason shook his head yes, and he loaded the conversation and the Skype episode.

"You handled yourself well and this girl is a mess … not a girl to associate with. She is doing this to make you do something stupid or she has a prank for you. Girls like this get together to pull pranks on guys like us. I admit she is a looker. If and when you decide to have sex, PROMISE me you will let me know, and I will get you condoms. I will show you how to use them then." Corey did the father/son talk since his wasn't here.

Jason said, "Thanks that means a lot! Don't think I will talk to any more girls until school starts. It just gets so lonesome."

"Here is something else you need to know. When you are married, you don't have to wear them. The wise girl has enough sense to be on the pill," and he shadowboxed Jason.

Roscoe told Guy about the situation at THE HOTEL. Adam wants us to intervene so he doesn't get in trouble. They swung by the hotel to view the security tape of who was with the man named Lonnie. and Guy freaked out. "Those three are the deadliest cons. Print out their pictures and I will run them through the databases, quick as I can! So we will know everything we need to know. This is going down soon. I'll be back. Be safe. Text Adam not to do anything by himself."

Guy was out of there. Back at the GM & GS Private Investigation Service office, he showed Tate how to process it and it started printing out.

"Dag gone they have rap sheets longer than this table!"

"If you see them Tate, go the other way … promise! I am calling in the big dogs."

Guy called Trevor and told him he was faxing over the three profiles, and needed him to get the SBI and FBI back ASAP!

The team was on the way. Marcus's team needed this information, too! He called Marcus to fax him the photos and rap sheets. He told him these men are planning a heist of THE HOTEL or THE CASINO. He did not know which, but his bodyguards needed to know because these men are dangerous.

Adam was in with Marcus at the time of the call. Marcus said. "You and Janice are not to go back to work for ANY reason. Get her on the phone, I will tell her. I need to tell her."

"Thank you, she is a handful," he could not find her. She had left a note going to get the dry cleaning. Be back soon!

He was pacing, it just didn't feel right. So he ask Corey had Ellen seen Janice ... and the answer was no.

He called her cell and she didn't answer.

She was in traffic and could not call. She was on her way back home when a van sideswiped her and turned her car upside down, and it rolled over the embankment. She was penned inside.

Adam could not stay at the house. He had to find her … and there she was in the car upside down. They were using the JAWS OF LIFE to get her out. He ran as fast as he could, and the police were waving him back. "But that is my wife! So get out of my way!"

"They will soon have her out, sir!" he went straight to her and with one hank had her in his arms running when the car blew up.

He took her to the ambulance, "Please help her. Do something. Please HURRY!"

"You can follow us to the hospital or you can go ahead and we will be there by that time," the EMT said.

He got on Corey's bike that he had borrowed, and was standing in the emergency room, and saw the same guy. He waved him in and he didn't have to deal with the ER desk.

Those EMTs knew if they didn't let him back there with them, he would probably tear the ER up, and they were right.

He called Marcus and told him to tell everyone.

"Sir, we are going to have to take her into surgery. She is bleeding internally. She is stabilized and you can go with us. We will show you where the surgical waiting room is ... and they can get you something to drink. It may be awhile. We will keep you posted." "Can I kiss her?" Adam asked.

He walked as fast as they, and they stopped at the door, and he kissed her and said, "I love you Janice, fight for us." Then he walked and sat down holding his head with both hands.

"I don't pray much .... but they tell me you can help, if I ask! Help her recover. Amen!"

"Hey there! Give me a hug," Madeline hugged him tight as did Debbie. Madeline and Trevor had heard it on the scanner.

Trevor said, "I got to do this business here so you and Debbie go be with Adam. Tate and I will be on later!"

They got coffee and sodas and candy bars. They didn't know if he had eaten, and it was going to be awhile.

Adam wasn't one to chitchat, so he walked the halls and could not sit or stand still. He knew the baby was gone, but he prayed some more that she would make it through. He had been so worried that she might get shot, he never dreamed a car wreck may take her from him.

Six hours later, the doctor came out and confirmed that the baby died. "She has a broken pelvis and one punctured lung, but all has been done that we could do. Her vital signs are stable. The next 48 to 72 hours she will be in the ICU. We will keep you posted." Adam gave him his cell number and was told he could only see her every hour for ten minutes and 8:00PM was the last visitation. He could come back at nine tomorrow and as long as she was in ICU, the ten minutes was all they could allow. He shook the doctor's hand and said, "THANK YOU take care of her. I'LL BE OUT HERE."

Madeline walked with him and he stopped and she held him. He cried on her shoulder, "I've never loved anyone like I have loved, Janice. She has loved me, how I don't know. We lost our baby!"

This is when Madeline started crying. Trevor and Tate came in. They didn't say anything, and Debbie filled them in that Janice was in recovery and would at some point be moved to the ICU.

They talked him into going to getting a bite to eat and Madeline said, "The doctor or nurse will call you, Adam. No matter where you are. You can't get sick. You have to be strong for her. She's going to need you in the coming days."

"You are right! I haven't eaten, but that candy bar since yesterday and you 'all need to eat something."

They went to the cafeteria and he ate very little, but did eat something which was better than eating nothing at all.

Tate had never seen his brother cry in his whole entire life. He would be in the same fix, if it were Debbie.

When they got back to the waiting room, it was on the news that the man driving the truck that hit Janice was being charged with DUI.

"It could have been anyone of us," Trevor said. "Drunk drivers don't have a clue how many people they hurt!"

CHAPTER TWO

Roscoe had the FBI at Trevor's and SBI at Madeline's old house, just like before Trevor called Lonestar. The team was preparing for battle. "These characters will never leave the premises. We will nab them so swiftly, and take them out."

"We got to get them in the act so the conviction will stick," the agent said.

Roscoe said, "Wouldn't it be nice if we could before hand, but the law says they are innocent until proven guilty. These three were not even innocent when they were born."

Guy said, "Bro she was pregnant and lost the baby. Adam is going crazy ... but he and she at least will not be in THE CASINO when this goes down."

Marcus and Eunice were headed for the hospital. Corey and Ellen would stay with Jason. Eunice hugged her nephew and held his face, "She's in good hands. These doctors are wonderful."

Marcus hugged him and Adam wouldn't let him go. Marcus just held him, and patted him on the back. Eunice was now crying. Her brother, Chris had never been a father to either of the boys. They had no clue what a real father was until now. Her husband, her amazing husband, Marcus was making up for lost time. She loved him more each day.

Little did Eunice know, but her boys and her nephews had made him... be a better man. Until Eunice, he had never cared who he stepped on as long as they were making him money.

Days went by and Sunday arrived and Lonnie was fidgety.

The other two, Rocky the squirrel and the Iceman were calm, cool, and collected. "Any questions?" Lonnie asked.

Rocky had his high powered rifle that would blast through any bullet proof glass. He had bought it in Brazil ... purchased at a mafia house sale. He laughed a sadistic sound and said, "MY BABY is ready! Ain't she pretty!" He could break her down and put her back together in 38 seconds. "Been practicing like those racer car teams ... down to the seconds." He was proud of his evil accomplishment.

The Iceman had two semi-automatic pistols from the heart of Mexico. The rapid firing mechanism was a sight to behold and he wielded them to perfection. Lonnie was to distract the man with the bag and take him hostage. His switchblade was less noticeable, and his Beretta was in his waistband. Italian made to kill. He liked to brag that he was an Italian stallion, but it was a joke amongst his gang.

"Okay you are creeping me out. Sit Lonnie. Sit!" The Iceman had spoken, so he sat. "We got all night!"

Lonestar had arrived and told Trevor he was going to check out the rooftops of both buildings to let his men know. The teams knew him from last time, but he may need to remind Marcus's men to review his appearance.

Between the two buildings, the hotel was higher and he could see the casino entrance better. He could see the hotel entrance better so he was set for the duration. The element of surprise was how he like to put it. He had his night vision scope on. If it went down in the daytime, it was even better.

The SBI and the FBI knew his location. As he got set, the Brinxx truck arrived. Lonestar knew this was it, if they were going to do a robbery. The driver got out and the other man locked the door from the inside.

Rocky was walking in the parking lot, and so was The Iceman. They were mingling with the crowd. The teams were in place. The people leaving were almost to their cars.

When the driver came out to load the bags, Lonnie had put the Beretta in his side. The inside man kept the door locked.

"Lonnie said, "Tell him to open or we will blow him away." He refused and Rocky shot a hold in the side window and the man inside unlocked it. The FBI waited for Lonestar's move and he popped Lonnie, and they fired and killed both Rocky and The Iceman at the same time before either could pull a trigger.

"Good work men. All of three seconds!" Roscoe said. The two Brinxx men were safe and the money was intact.

"Three menaces of society have been eliminated," Guy said and patted his brother on the back. "Feels like old times."

"That was well planned," one of Marcus's guards said, "I' ll report to the boss that you guys saved him a million dollars."

"WOW that's more than I will make in a lifetime," Roscoe said. "You guys come on over to Trevor's and we will have some breakfast."

Marcus came up about that time, "They're busy, still at the hospital. It's my treat follow me to the casino buffet!"

Roscoe walked in and Beatrice came running, "Don't run you might drop something! I'm am in no condition to pick those triplets up and put them back!"

"I was so worried. I saw it on the news and when I heard no one was hurt except the robbers. The babies stopped kicking me. I can't say how relieved I am that you are home safe."

She kissed him and sat to get her breath, "These babies are heavy! Got to get me one of those mobility scooters! I saw a little old lady the other day and thought I might just mug her because I needed it more than she," Beatrice was talking a mile a minute and she covered her mouth.

"I will catch a few winks and you can talk all you want to. Okay?" Roscoe rubbed the triplets. Would you like me to put the triplets to bed?" he asked.

"Would you and I'll just sit right here!" she smiled.

"I'm glad you haven't lost your sense of humor. After these triplets, I think seven is a good number and my wife can get her girlish figure back, and I can be neutered, and we can have some real fun when I get home. What do you think about that?"

"You must be really tired. Go to bed. You are really really talking crazy, honey!" Beatrice said.

"It comes with the territory. Night dear!" Roscoe walked toward the bedroom.

She said, "I'll be in there to tuck you in, in a few minutes!"

"Don't you dare! Leave me be!" he said. "Well for two hours anyway," he winked and shut the door.

The ICU had called for visitation to start and Adam was first in line to press the button. Madeline went with him and he was not prepared. She was on a ventilator, and

IVs in both arms, drainage tubes everywhere, pee catheter, and three machines beeping and recording stuff. He held her hand and it was ice cold.

Her face was cut up on the left side and she was so still. He said, "I love you baby. I'm here!" and her B/P shot up. He said, "Relax you don't have to talk! Just rest and get well!" Her B/P went back to normal. "Everything is going to be all right. We will get through this together. I will come every chance that they will let me!"

He kissed her cold hand because he was afraid to kiss her forehead. He might hit something and the nurse said the rails had to be up at all times.

Then the ten minutes was up. Madeline had not spoken, she was just there for Adam. Janice's eyes were closed the whole visit.

He turned to Madeline and said, "Thank you for being here for me."

"You are welcome. That's what family is for. Your Aunt will be here today. Jason is old enough to come to the hospital. If you get a chance ... watch the news. Trevor and I are going on home when Eunice gets here, and we'll be back tonight."

He sat and watched the news. The robbery was at the casino and Marcus was being interviewed and he thanked everyone that helped in getting these three men off the street.

Kyleigh ran and jumped in Guy's arms. "I am so glad you are home! I saw the news! It was awful! They are dead, the mean people are all dead! I am good, honey. Really I am!"

She did not sound like herself, so they may need to get an appointment with her doctor. It had been almost four years. She still was having flashbacks when anything was reported, and the reporters say these were EVIL people. She freaks out. The doctor said she may always have flashbacks or no flashbacks. "The brain has to heal in its own time."

He kissed her and as long as she responded that was a good thing. It was when she shutdown that he could not bear it.

Madison came in, "Daddy Daddy is home. Mommy! Daddy is home." They had breakfast and Guy went to lie down for a couple of hours.

Bruce and Jana had called to check on Unitus and Adriana.

They filled them in on Janice and Adam. They told them the inside scoop of the robbery. The little Vanderbilt was learning to use his lungs and Unitus said, "He has lungs like his ….. father." He almost messed up and said mother.

She smiled at him, she was feeling better, but he had four more weeks and she was unnerving him.

"Come here honey let me …" Adriana said.

"Don't you dare come near me. Angel is in her room playing and the boy wants to play," Unitus said.

"I know and I was going to play with him, but you won't let me!" She wiggled her finger, "Come to mama play is all we can do," they watched both monitors as they played.

Tate stayed with Adam when Eunice or Madeline couldn't.

She was out of ICU and it still was pitiful to watch her try to talk or move. Physical therapy was in everyday.

"Torturing her," Adam said. Madeline reassured him that it was necessary with a broken pelvis. The drainage tube was out of her lung. With the fluid gone in her lung, she was able to talk better and breath better.

The weeks went by and now school was starting soon.

Jason was excited to go to school this year and who was the first girl he saw. Yes, Cheri must have changed schools or was she going to this school all along.

Corey said girls like her like to play pranks, but she was not going to get to him this year.

She was eyeballing him and rubbed her pencil between her breasts, and he quickly went into the bathroom to call Corey.

"I might need them," he stated.

Corey said, "Need what? What are you talking about?"

"Them! She is here at my school this year and she is already rubbing her tits at me! You got to come and get me. I can't walk down the hall like this. Tell mom you got to get me. I spilled a drink on my clothes and I have to change. Do it for me, Corey!" Jason just keep washing his hands and standing close to the sink until the bell rang and he walked out the front door and waited by a tree for Corey.

"Waiting for somebody. Hope it is me that you want to skip school with," Cheri walked in front of him. "What you got under that book. Let me see!"

He said, "Go away! You don't bother me!"

"Oh I am not trying … but if I did try you would be REAL bothered," and she backed him up against the tree.

About that time Corey came up on his bike and she just stood there while Jason and his boner hopped on the back.

"That the one," Corey asked.

"Yep and she wants me bad. I have this to walk around with. What am I going to do Corey!"

"You are going to ask mom ... if you can go to a private school that someone is picking on you and you can't defend yourself," Corey said and added, "You don't have to tell her. IT's a girl!"

"She is a looker," Corey said teasing him.

"You've said that twice so if you are not going to get me the condoms, then shut up! Already!"

"NO need, the next school can be an all boys school," Corey was still up to mischief.

"Just whose side are you on anyways!" Jason now had to face the music because mom was at the door.

"WE gotta have a serious talk Mom, but first I got to change clothes," Jason said.

Corey said, "Go easy on him. He's had a hard day already!"

"I'm gonna get you for that Corey! Not cool! Not cool at all!" Jason said.

"I need to change schools. I've got a girl trying her best to get in my pants and you and I don't want that! Do we Mom?" honesty is NOT the best policy. Eunice almost fainted.

CHAPTER THREE

Adam finally was able to bring Janice home after four weeks, and the physical therapist would be in three times a week Monday Wednesday and Friday at two PM. That was set in stone.

The doctor said for two more weeks only light activity. He put her on an antidepressant due to losing the baby, and loss of mobility most people suffer from depression. That may help and she may not need it. Just keep me posted. If one doesn't work, we can try another.

Janice was so happy to be going home. Adam had been with her every day, and was making her feel loved and cherished.

She was told not to have sex for two more weeks. She was hoping when she laid beside him that he would still want her broken body.

He assured her he wanted everything. He loved everything about her. She was walking very slow and that thrilled him to see her walk. She had not been able to for so long.

They had not talked about the loss of the baby and neither wanted that conversation anytime soon. They just wanted to be alone.

He toted her into the house so she did not have that long walk, and she wrapped her arms around his neck, and kissed him behind his ear.

"Honey, don't do that I might drop you. He stood her up in their room. For the first time, he could not have her. So he let her do whatever she wanted to do.

"I just want to lay here beside my husband and look at you, and sleep till noon without someone waiting me up for vital signs."

"I just want to lay here and look at you, and kiss you, and I love you being home. I was so worried that you weren't coming home anytime soon. The doctor said you did remarkable."

"I did well because you made me. You willed me to live when I had given up. I did not want to come home to you an invalid."

"I married you in sickness and health," Adam said.

"Now let's sleep for a little while unless you are hungry?"

"I'm tired. Let's sleep," and he laid his arm across her and then drew it back. "Did I hurt you?"

"No it would hurt, if you didn't want to hold me. Hold me all you want to," she was smiling at him like she use to do.

He closed his eyes and dreamed of how they use to make passionate love and they would again. He just needed to give her time.

She was crying inside because the doctor said she "may not be able to have another child. It just depends on how your body heals itself. Everything was repaired and looks good. When you two begin your sexual activity just go slow and let everything stretch slowly back to where it should be. You will know. If it hurts, stop. Then try again later. Sound good?"

"Yes, it sounds great. I thought I may never be able to!"

Ellen and Debbie came and spent half a day pampering her. They did her nails and her hair. Shaved her legs and she felt like a new woman.

"You two are just the best friends a girl could ever have. I love you for it. One day I will pay you back," Janice said.

Adam came in, "Wow don't you look nice. You two can come back anytime, except call first!" and he laughed and he was waving them out.

"That was rude. You threw them out!" Janice said with a twinkle in her eyes.

"Damn straight!" and he walked to the bathroom and stripped his clothes off.

"I want to hold you and make love to you. It's been six weeks, but who's counting?" he grinned.

He took her breath away, "The doctor said we need to go slow for a couple of times. Do you think that thing has a slow button?"

"OH baby! I love it when you talk dirty to me," Adam said.

"Then bring it over here and pick me up and I'll see what it'll do." He started rubbing her legs. "They feel good. Your hair smells like lavender even your tits taste like lavender. How did you do that?" he asked.

"It's called a bubble bath. You can help me in and out next time," she purred as he was setting her on fire and he knew it.

"Baby I got to," he moaned. She was so ready just like old times. He was going so careful. She was stretching and grimacing. Everything worked."It'll be even better next time."

Beatrice said, "Wake up honey! It's time!"

Roscoe mumbled, "Not again honey, I've got a headache!"

She took her pillow and swatted him, "It's time! Get the suitcase and take me to the hospital unless you want to deliver them!"

"OH my stars! Let me help you. Sit right here and I will dress. Call Mrs April and Mrs Bloomingdale!" He was so excited he ran into the wall.

"Did you hurt yourself honey! Be careful. I need you today!" mumbling to herself. "I need you everyday."

The nanny was here and asked, "Is there anything I can do?"

"Just take care of my babies and maybe call me a cab. Just joking, honey!" as Roscoe came around the corner.

"I am a very good driver under normal conditions, but I can't promise to drive slow … and if you scream I may run off the road a bit, but I am ready!" they walked to the van and he asked if she wanted to lay down.

"No that is how I got these triplets!" and Beatrice smiled sweetly. Her pale green eyes sparkling.

"I love you mother of my children," and off they went.

He called his police buddy and he escorted them in with the blue lights flashing.

"Have you called that nurse we like?" she asked.

"NO! We have been a little busy. I will call her in a few, dear," Roscoe had her in a wheelchair and called the number.

"The triplets are arriving at their destination!" he hung up.

Adriana was calling Marcus, "I was watching TV and saw you. Why didn't you call me and Unitus?"

"Honey, it all happened so fast and you 'all were safe and needed to take care of the babies. Everyone's fine here," Marcus was explaining and he should have called.

"I will if ever you are in danger honey. Forgive this time," he added.

"This time only! I only have but one daddy, and you are him. I love you daddy! Kiss Eunice for me!" and she hung up.

"Mr Universe did you know?" she was rolling her eyes at Unitus who just came into the room.

He was in trouble when she called him that.

"That's not my name. It is Honey, Darling, Sweetums, Big Guy, Big Boy!" he was smiling at her.

"Point well taken counselor," she was wiggling her finger to come there, and he was definitely running to her.

"Can I approach the bench?" he asked.

"I would be glad to hear your case Unitus versus Armed Robbery at the said wife father's place of business! Proceed."

He knelt by her so that Angel could climb up him like a monkey bar and hang while he lifted his little girl, and made her giggle.

"Order in the court!" and Adriana looked at the monitor. Vanderbilt was fast asleep.

"I did not know either Madame Judge of mine!"

"Do you have any evidence to bring before the court that proves you are indeed innocent of alleged non action?"

Unitus said, "I do your honor. I was making mad passionate love to my wife, and in no condition to see or hear any reports of a robbery at my father-in-law's place of business. I can provide the said nightgown in the hamper as evidence."

"That will not be necessary! This judge frees you on the condition that you will always have this as your excuse for any wrong doing. Mr Universe, this is a matter that I would like to review in my chambers at said ten PM. Is that clear or do you need an escort?"

"Your Honor, I am a repeat offender. I need to be handcuffed. Can that be arranged? Or fined repeated with your long arm of the law!" He was drooling and she was in his face.

"Oh Honey, I ain't gonna make it to the ten o'clock judgment. Do you concur?" she nodded with glee at the judge's sentencing to 8 PM. Angel will be down for the count.

"I agree thank you for your mercy! MERCY I hope I make it till then!" He smiled rolling on the floor with Angel to tire her out. He bathed her while Adriana breastfed Vanderbilt and played with him until he tired, and fell asleep. She was pain free and her suture line was tight. Her strongest body again!

Unitus joined her in the shower and took her breath away.

He was devouring her mouth. "I really needed to wash my artificial leg tonight. You know how to do it better than I." He knew it was a lame excuse for him to shower with her." She knew how to make everything better for him!

Marcus had called Tate and Debbie over for dinner with he and Eunice. Of course Jason, Corey and Ellen, Adam and Janice joined the family affair.

"I have asked you all here to celebrate Janice's full recovery and to ask a certain young woman to join my Master chef at THE CASINO's exclusive dining quarters.

Debbie I hope you will accepted this apprenticeship position and rise to the top. Now let's eat!" Debbie was so stunned that happy tears were running down her face.

Jason said, "Mom! Mom! She is crying!"

Eunice said, "She's okay. Those are happy tears!"

Tate hugged her and kissed her hair, "I knew it! You are the best, and you can learn from the best. You have wanted to go to a real culinary school especially that one in New York. So you decide? Either way is fine with me!"

"You have your new job and now I will have my dream job. It would be foolish to move away from the people we love. Mr. Buchanan I will take it!" and she smiled from ear to ear.

He gave her the thumbs up sign and continued eating. The man did loved to eat. He loved his new family and extended family more each day.

"Call in the morning and ask to speak to Chief Henri and tell him I recommended you. You two can decide on where and when you start. Call me if you have any problems," and the dessert was served.

They all said, "Here! Here!"

CHAPTER FOUR

Michelle was now a strawberry blonde and she NEVER wore black. Her past was black as a "Raven" and never to resurface again. She was toting her art pad and overflowing shoulder bag to the library where she was going to study a particular artist's designs for class, when a handsome gentleman bumped into her.

All her supplies and new makeup went onto the floor. She was scrambling to pick them up especially her tampon.

He was helping and said, "I am so sorry love. I wasn't watching where I was going."

His British accent made her look up into the most beautiful brown eyes with golden specks, and smoking hot body. His shirt stretched across a taut set of abs. She could not miss them as he stood up. Looking down at her holding out his hand to help her up, he said, "May I interest you in a cup of tea?"

"That would be nice. My fave is Darjeeling, but only if you promise not to empty my purse again!" and they laughed.

She had been taking etiquette classes and trying to learn to control her temper. She must be getting better at it because in the past, she would have cold-cocked him up beside his head.

She smiled as she walked to a nearby cafe in her three inch Louboutin brown heels that matched her brown shoulder bag. She laid her art tablet on the table and hung her purse on the chair turning with her mini dress rising to reveal her long long slender legs. The same legs that she had always kept hidden under black leather pants.

This was her new image and her new life that was a complete opposite of her past identity. That was the only way she would be able to survive. Her only thought after Haruto died was, "I don't want him to have died for nothing."

The Madeline woman was her light that she saw before she went to bed at night. She cares about me. She had never had anyone to truly care.

She had been kicked around by her family, both verbally and sexually abused as a child. When she turned sixteen, she said no more and left. She had lived on the streets and it had hardened her to the core, and no one ever messed with her unless she let them.

Looking across the table a man was smiling back at her, and their hot tea was being served. She also had learned to bat her eyelashes and she asked, "What brings you to the states or do you live here?"

She was still too blunt. To put it delicately, she just wanted to know with whom she was conversing. She smiled, but not at him particularly, but at how corny she sounded. Her instructor would have been "delighted" with her progress.

He said, "Here for a convention, love. I tend to bump into people I want to get to know. I confess I am attracted to you!"

Talking about being blunt, this dude has got me beat. She sipped her tea wishing she could turn it up, and haul tail.

It being hot tea, she just sipped with her pinkie high in the air and said, "You do have a way of knocking a girl off her feet!" and she batted those new false eyelashes that were the rage now.

He was drowning in her eyes and getting warmer under the collar, so he loosened his tie. Between those lashes and that miniskirt that had ridden to her crotch, he was having a time with his libido ... usually that was not a problem.

"I do apologize once again. I was looking at the statue in front of the library, and it reminded me of my father. Clearly I was at fault. I am glad if I had to run into someone, I am glad it was a beautiful lass as yourself!"

The man is a con artist, and talks a load of crap with every phrase he is pitching. She smiled, "Thank you for the tea and I take it as a compliment. No more can I tarry. I have a class I must attend. Toodles!" She was out the door before he could stand and pay the bill.

She ducked into the nearby clothing store and hid in the bathroom. She tried on a few clothes. When she came out in her new navy slacks and navy and white long sleeved shirt,

he was there propped on the side of an Aston Martin staring at her. She swung her hair to the side, and marched on with her over-sized purse and packages in hand.

"May I help you with those? I promise to be a gentleman and not drop them or your purse," he smiled. His teeth were perfect and his chin was chiseled, not her type.

This man is getting on my nerves. He had better stop or else. "No I am fine. Really I am!" She hailed a cab and got in.

Madeline and Trevor had opted out of the party at Marcus and Eunice's for Debbie, and would celebrate the news with her and Tate when they got home.

Madeline had purchased her a new styled chef's hat and Trevor had her a piece of money for any utensils that she might need.

Bruce and Jana had also, gotten her a gift. A new apron for the house that said, "Master of cooking" and packaging it with a bottle of red Rose wine.

Tate and Debbie came tiptoeing into a dark house. Then the lights went on, "Surprise!"

She could not believe this night! It had been so special for her in every way.

Tate and she celebrated this day in a personal way that night that was worth more to her than any of the material gifts. He held her and spoke his love. They were blissfully entwined till the wee hours of the morning.

He arose first, "Get up sleepyhead, and make me some breakfast Master Chef!"

She stretched and said, "I thought I already had!" and grinned from under the covers.

"Aah yes you did and a mighty fine breakfast it was!" he dove back into bed.

"You know I am going to be LATE for work," Tate stated.

"Complain Complain," Debbie rubbed his bare chest.

"I have no complaints here. I will take my tongue lashing from Guy gladly. It will be worth it!" he kissed her deeply.

The Aston Martin had followed her to her apartment building. He had to know where she lived. "Damn! I am stalking this girl! What is wrong with me?"

He turned the car around and went back to his hotel where he poured himself a Scotch said, "Get it together old boy! She is not worth getting arrested for …or is she!" he laughed.

"No woman is!" and he poured over the papers for his lecture. His thoughts kept going back to that strawberry blonde. She had magnificent legs. "Stop! You probably will never see her again and you will be gone in a week. Why start something you cannot finish!"

He looked out across the city and the bright lights. He would be in another city with bright lights next week, and the week after. Always in demand. Aerodynamics was his field of expertise. The latest technology and the demonstrations were what he got paid big bucks to do.

As a lad he studied at Eton, and joined the Royal Air Force and paid his dues. Just now was he reaping the benefits of hard work. Why would he jeopardize it all for a woman?

Because he was lonely, he surmised. Yes, he had hoped by now that he would be married or have a companion that would travel with him, and share in his passion for adventure.

There were none of the women he had met thathad any motive, but greed. None had a brain cell that connected, except to his wallet. He walked away from the window and turned on the TV, and it was advertising an Art Show in town to be held this weekend. There she was standing by an illustration, deep in the crowd. He spotted her. She was an artist … a student. She had been honest about a class, she had to attend. Now he knew it was an art class.

"Man, you are so horny. You are not in your right mind, if you think this beautiful woman is going to give you anymore of her time... if she finds out you are basically a salesman."

Yes, a very high priced salesman.

"Robert Einstein is here to speak to us." She was listening and preparing to take notes of this required lecture for her class. It was an aerodynamic design that she was suppose to sketch, and write a paper on by Monday.

She looked up, and there he was as the guest speaker. His voice was hypnotizing her. She felt herself being drawn into a fantasy of her past sexual experiences, and pure raw desire. So she stood up and walked out. Not worth the extra credit for her class grade, if it was going to disrupt the solitude that she had found in her art.

Disrupt her celibacy. She walked fast to the subway and entered her apartment with a pat on her back from herself. That was a good move. Now think not of that man ever again.

"Hello, I didn't get your name? I have to ask why you walked out of my lecture a week ago?" Robert asked.

She was standing pretending not to recognize him, but it wasn't working. She was walking toward the subway.

"We had tea last week," he smiled.

Damn him, he was a pushy stiff.

"Oh yes. I got a call and didn't want the phone to disrupt your lecture, so I left to meet my fiancee`," that should shut him down.

She got on the subway and it was crowded.

He got on also. Standing so close, she could feel his breath on the back of her neck. He breathed in her CIARA perfume.

"But you don't have a ring on. What about me compels you to lie, love? Do I wreck your nerves like you are wrecking mine?" The train lurched forward and he grabbed her waist to steady her, and she made a mistake and turned. The people beside her pushed her into him as they were getting off.

She was wearing another mini with an over-sized sweater and no bra. So when she pressed against his white stiff shirt, he could feel she was aroused. Her hard nipples were rubbing his chest as the train lurched again.

That was it! He had to take a chance and he kissed her trembling lips, and it had been so long that she responded, and sucked his tongue. She was breathing erratically, and grabbed her purse to put between them.

"That is a good idea! I want to nibble on every inch of you, but these people are watching!" he said staring into her eyes.

This famous lecturer had made a move on her and boy did he want her. His erection was still imprinted on her thigh.

She closed her eyes and held her head back and licked her lips. He was savoring her face, and had to have her.

She opened her eyes and shook her head, "I am not a one night stand. So go elsewhere! Please go elsewhere!" knowing if he did it again she would fall right back into his arms, and make a scene and possible a fool of herself.

"I don't want to go elsewhere or I would not be here on this gosh awful train! LUSTING after you, love." She got off. He didn't!

He had to leave the following day, but not before he got her name from her doorman. "Michelle ... Tell her Robert will see her in a week at the cafe at twelve!" he gave him a hundred dollar bill to assure that he would tell her.

"My good man I will match it, if you tell me her last name?"

"Can't do that sir, but if she wants to see you. She will tell you a week from today at the cafe at noon!" the doorman said.

"Fair enough!" and he shook his hand.

Michelle went to her class shaking and hypervigilant all day. Fearing, he would pop up at any minute. He tasted so good and smelled so good. She wanted him. That was her old self talking, and be damn if she was going backwards. To do so, would be disastrous.

"Michelle! Michelle! I was asked to give you a message from a gentleman by the name of Robert," and the doorman gave her the message.

"He will be disappointed in a week at the cafe at noon! I am not going to go anywhere out of my apartment," she told herself. "On next Wednesday or Thursday or Friday! That should make it clear to him that I am not interested." But I am interested in him. Damn it!

So much that she looked his profile up on the computer. Robert Einstein well known lecturer for the Aerodynamic Company … blah blah blah listing all his attributes. Not listed was that he had brown eyes with gold specks, and soft massive hands that made her blood boil with the heat that penetrated to her core.

I must concentrate on my studies and make Madeline and Trevor proud of me, and proud of myself for once. She did just that and excelled, and did not think of this Robert fellow anymore.

He... on the other hand … was obsessed with her. He found out where the art school was and poured through the names of the students finding only one student by the name of Michelle. Pulling up her picture, it was her. Now he had a name and would not interfere again until her graduation.

That would be the day he would woo her and possess her. That was a given. Never had he allowed a woman to control his every thought like she did, in such a short amount of time. It was her spunk, passion, and drive to succeed at her craft that was so attractive.

Then that kiss ... so passionate that he ached thinking about it! If she did not want him after graduation, then he would not pursue her anymore. He had to try one more time or regret it for the rest of his life.

The nurse met them at the ER with a very large wheelchair.

"I wanted you to be comfortable, so I came for my triplets in style. This is your chariot madame," pointing to the wheelchair. "The doctor is waiting and the nursery has been prepared for the babies."

"Have you been talking to my wife lately sounds like this was planned?" Roscoe chuckled.

The nurse says, "She calls me every week OOPS! I shouldn't have told. My bad!" and she walked while Roscoe pushed the wheelchair.

Beatrice yelled, "Stop you forgot the suitcase!"

"I'll get it later! Got to get me some triplets first! Kiss Kiss," he kissed her.

The nurse said, "We don't have time for this!"

"Oh we have time, he promised me something else!"

Beatrice was rolling her eyes at him.

"You can't be serious!" he said. "I can't perform under these circumstances! Beatrice I draw the line! Anything, but that!"

"Okay you can kiss my feet when we get to the delivery room," she said.

"You got a deal! Shooey that was close!" wiping his brow.

The nurse came back, "What have you done to my Roscoe? He is all sweaty. You are NOT going to pass out on me THIS time. Are you? I better go get the machine and check your blood sugar. It may have dropped," she went scurrying off.

"Beatrice are you in pain?" Roscoe was concerned. She had been laughing so hard she was crying.

Big crocodile tears, and she couldn't get her breath.

"Speak to me, honey! Doctor! Nurse! She is in pain. Do something!"

She had hiccups and a contraction hit her. "Holy cow! That was three times as worse as the last one."

"Cross your legs dear! There's no one out here that can deliver," Roscoe was in panic mode.

"One I could deliver honey, but three I CANNOT! The doctor is getting a small fortune to deliver our babies, so I'll be right back!"

He went to the desk, "Overhead that doctor, NOW or else!" Roscoe demanded.

"Or else what Mr. Smith?" the smart mouth young nurse at the desk asked.

"Or else I will pick her up and lay her on this desk and you can deliver my babies! Is that clear, Missy?"

"High aye, sir!" she overhead the doctor and he came running.

Beatrice said, "Doc they are on their way and I haven't pushed yet! They must have a mind of their own!"

"OK girls! Let's get a move on it. NOW!" the doctor said.

Into the delivery room they went with no time to spare.

They started coming ten minutes later, and the older nurse got Roscoe a chair. He was looking pale and his blood sugar was 70. She took a candy bar out of her uniform pocket and gave it to him.

"He can't eat it in here!" the young nurse said.

The older nurse said, "This man's blood sugar has dropped and he is over six feet tall. Can YOU pick him up? Because I sure can't!"

"Oh!" she says, "Eat Mr. Smith! Eat!"

FIRST comes Johnny.

SECOND comes Jill.

THIRD comes Jessie.

Two girls and one boy!

"Yeah, Team! All are doing fine!"

"The father's not doing so hot!" said the doctor. I'm going to cut the cords because you sir are in no condition!"

Roscoe nodded.

"I know Doc, but I have one thing I have to do. Can you hold this candy bar while I do it!" Roscoe said to the young nurse.

"Sure" and Roscoe got up, straighten his clothes and walked up to Beatrice as if to kiss her, then went to the foot of the bed and as promised kissed her feet!"

"It takes a real man to do that!" the young nurse said.

The older nurse slapped her on the back and said, "Honey that's the first thing we have agreed on all day!"

Guy was waiting for Tate to show up at the office and he got a call from Kyleigh, "Beatrice has had the triplets!"

"J J & J … two girls and one boy. Jill and Jessie, and little Johnny! They are exhausted. Your brother is a basket case."

"Why?" Guy asked.

"He thought he was going to have to deliver them and it terrified him. You need to check on him," Kyleigh stated.

"Okay I will!" Guy hung up.

"Bro, a little bird told me you had some news. What's up?"

"Guy stop. I've had a bad day. I may strangle you!" Roscoe said.

"What did I do?" Guy asked.

"Nothing that's the problem. I needed help and you were not there!"

"Did you call me? Let me check. No you did not … so now you think I have ESP. Hmm Heard that before!" Guy jested.

"What can I do to make your life easier?" Guy continued.

"Go suck an egg!" Roscoe said growling.

"Okay then what?" Guy asked again.

"Go over to the house and play with the twins. I am here for a long while," Roscoe begged.

"Okay, Kyleigh and I will do. What else?" Guy scratched his head.

"Kiss your wife because I'm going to go and kiss mine. Bye later!" and he hung up.

Guy still had the phone in hand when Kyleigh came around the corner, "Kyleigh, he wants me to kiss you and make mad passionate love to you!"

Her eyes squinted, "Roscoe said that?"

"NO, but he did say to kiss you! He has a request of us," Guy said.

"That I strip down right now! HUH?" she laughed because Guy was getting into his here I come stance.

"NO, that he is staying and wants us to check on the kids. But I like your interpretation of his message much better!"

Michelle was not at the cafe on Wednesday at noon and Robert was disappointed. He left with respect for her decision and wouldn't seek her out any more. He walked by her apartment and told the doorman just that, so she would not have to worry. "I UNDERSTAND HER DECISION. SHE'S JUST NOT INTERESTED."

He had no idea that she saw him from her window, and definitely his assessment was completely the opposite. She was too interested that was the problem.

Six months later …

Michelle was on the flight to see the Porters. At the Charlotte Airport, she ran smack into a tall stranger. He grabbed her and held her close, her high heeled boots made them equal in height.

"You probably don't remember me," he said as she stared into his brown eyes with golden specks.

She swallowed and said, "I remember you well, Robert!"

"Michelle, I have thought of you often!" He still had her waist in a vice grip and no one could see under her cape, what he was doing. He didn't want to stop kneading her buttocks and drawing her even closer.

"Just like before your nipples are hard." He had taken one hand to feel them swell. Her breath was leaving her and she leaned forward.

"I see nothing has changed for you either. Your leg ornament is enticing" and placed her hand under her cape and rubbed it, to see if he would flinch, and he did.

He doubled over till their lips were kissing.

Neither remembered where they were until a man passing said, "Get a room!" and they parted.

Looking at each other in shock … both knew this was it!

"NO, I will not be a one night stand! Been there, done that and he is dead. Never again!" Michelle stared at Robert.

He said, "I don't want you one time! I know it would never be enough. I just want you to tell me what you want of me?"

She said, "I think you do, but I will tell you. I want you and all of you … each and every day and night and all in between.

I know you will not marry me... but I will NOT settle for less. Believe me I am worth it," and she proceed to show him.

He stood still and let her take him to another world, her hands under her cape unzipped and found him and cupped him gently and stroked till he was almost over the edge. Then she walked off and got in a white limo.

"Taxi! Taxi! Follow that limo wherever it goes! I will pay you double for your time!" Robert shouted.

Michelle could not believe he was following her.

She was dressed conservatively in a pair of stonewashed skinny jeans with a white off-the-shoulder sweater, and a caramel colored bulky cape. She had her strawberry blonde hair pulled up in a clasp. Large hoop earrings in the bottom piercing was a diamond at the base of a half moon, and the upper ear piercing had two stars.

"The Moon and Stars" was her signature design logo. She was looking forward to showing Madeline and Trevor. What were they going to think when she brings a man with her. This is not the homecoming that she had envisioned.

She closed her eyes until she saw the long white fence that led to Southfork.

She got out and leaned on the side of the limo staring at the approaching taxicab.

"What do you think you are doing?" Michelle asked.

"I lost you for six months. I have tried to get you out of my mind, but that is now impossible. You are right once will never be enough!" Robert stared back at her.

"Where are we?" he asked.

"At my home, you want to meet my family or do you want to leave? Your choice. I am going in!" and she walked toward the house.

He hesitated then he saw those long legs in the skinny jeans and those boots. It was happening, he was following her.

Madeline and Trevor, Tate and Debbie, and Bruce and Jana were all standing on the porch. A large banner was over the door, "WELCOME HOME MICHELLE!"

Madeline hugged her as did Trevor.

Madeline said, "Who do we have here?"

"Oh, just a man that followed me home. His name is Robert," Michelle shrugged her shoulders.

Trevor said, "I know Robert. How have you been?"

Michelle's mouth dropped open.

Robert said, "Close your mouth, darling!" and winked.

"Yes, we met years ago when he was piloting my personal aircraft. Tried my best to get him to work for me, but he had plans for an aerospace program. How did that go?"

"Ahem ..." Bruce said.

Trevor said, "Oh my goodness! Let's go in! This is Bruce, my son-in-law and his wife Jana. This is Tate, my son and his wife Debbie. The beautiful lady here is my wife,

Madeline. Michelle we adopted, and she has been away at art school, but you already know that … Welcome to our home!"

Madeline asked, "Robert how did you meet my Michelle?"

She quickly answered, "He was lecturing and my art show was next door, and we collided one day, and had a cup of tea! VOILA! Here we are!" she was staring at him and he at her.

"Collided is correct. Then she refused to have tea with me again. So I had to chase her here!"

They all laughed.

Trevor said, "That sounds like my Michelle."

"Let's get you two settled before supper," Madeline said.

"Tate show Robert and Michelle to their room … or do you want separate rooms?"

Robert said, "One room will be fine!" and grinned widely at Michelle.

Michelle rolled her eyes at him and they became beady.

Trevor asked, "Son, what are your intentions with my daughter?"

"Honorable, sir. I assure you we will pick out a ring tomorrow!"

"So you have proposed? Michelle didn't write anything about that," Trevor questioned.

"IT happened so suddenly. I think he needs to do it again in front of the family. So I can be totally SATISFIED … with my decision!" Michelle stated with a sweet smile.

He grabbed her hand, "Okay, Buttercup!"

He kissed her and took her breath away, and got down on one knee.

"Will you marry me tomorrow? Michelle… My Michelle?"

She had her mouth open.

Trevor repeated, "Close your mouth after you say yes!Quickly I am starving."

"I … I will." She was going to say no but she looked around and she wanted what they had. "I will be your wife Robert."

Then he kissed her thoroughly while everyone else, walked into the house.

"Now … I CAN'T walk in there. Look what you have done to me," Robert moaned.

"I'll let you wear my cape. The family will understand!" she said laughing.

"You shall pay for this lassie," he grinned.

"Is that another promise?" she quipped.

"Go pick out us a room and I will walk it off, and pay the cabbie."

He had totally forgotten about him.

"She does this to me every time. I don't know whether I am coming or going!" Robert explained handing him the cab fare.

The cab driver said, "That is love, amigo!"

She picked the one in the middle… away from all of them.

She could hardly eat, but she was smiling and her eyes never left Robert's.

Madeline said, "You lovebirds must be tired! We understand, if you want to retire early. Jet lag always gets to me!"

Robert pretend a yawn, "Me too, Mrs. Porter."

"Call me Madeline, please," and he nodded.

Michelle hugged everyone and told them how much she loved them.

She was walking down the hall in those skinny jeans in front of Robert, swaying those gorgeous seductive hips. When they got to the bedroom door, he was hard as a rock again.

Once inside the room, she began taking off her boots placing them in the closet. "This is mine and that side is yours." She unzipped her jeans. No undies and the sweater came off. No bra.

He had not moved.

He was staring with his mouth open!

"Shut your mouth Robert," she whispered.

She was beautiful. Perfectly proportioned! He had no idea how perfect until this moment. She was under all those big sweaters. GEEZ! I am going to make a fool out of myself!

He started unzipping and she immediately came to him and unbuttoned his shirt and felt this six foot two man's smooth muscular chest and shoulders, and hung the shirt up.

Returning to unbuckle and she was sitting him down, and he was kicking his expensive shoes off. She pulled his pants off and hung them up. His briefs were bulging and she was swooning.

"I cannot take them off yet … when I am your wife, I will. Until then, you will have to do it!"

"No problem. Come sit on my lap and tell me why you did not meet me that Wednesday?"

She straddled his briefs and he sucked in air. She put her hands on his shoulders, and began to wiggle slowly while kissing him thoroughly.

"Because this was going to happen and you knew it, too! I wanted to be sure it was me you wanted, not just a piece of ass," and she was rocking him and his briefs were getting wetter and wetter. He stood taking her with him, laying her on the bed, then removing the last of his clothing.

He began kissing her everywhere. She grabbed him and sucked his tongue as he went in "Oh Her Royal Majesty!

I can't stop! Come with me! Please," and she matched him while staring into his eyes.

He was grimacing. She was rising to meet him, quivering and vibrating. She said, "Just don't stop!"

He was doing it her way this time and he then stopped, "Say you love it!"

Her mouth was moving, but was saying, "Haruto, please! Do it now! Do it harder. I love you! Harder. Yes Baby, I love it so much! Don't ever stop!"

He was giving all he had and she climaxed. Then he did it harder, and she climaxed again. This time with him to the point of ecstasy.

He fell over on his back and stared at the ceiling.

"Who is Haruto?" Robert asked softly.

"NO worries. He's dead and now you know I had to get rid of that memory before tomorrow. You are mine to love and cherish. Is there a woman you need to get out of your head?"

Michelle had to know.

"No … I bed and leave. No ties ever! They chase me, like I chased you. No worries. You are all ... more than I ever imagined, and I am going to have to have you again!"

He was clinching his teeth to hold his load till she was ready, and she was working it up and down, and all around.

All around back up and pressed down, then it enveloped all of him.

"Give it to me fast and hard … the harder the better" and he did. "Harder please harder. Yes! You did it! I love you Robert! Do it till you can't do it anymore. I want every little drop that you have. I need need need oh yes! Now you are really doing it." They peaked together without holding anything back.

He lay there so sedated, he could hardly move.

"You are the best I have ever had, and you are mine now Michelle! No one else's EVER. I knew it, the first time I saw you!"

She finally admitted, "I knew you were the one, but I wasn't ready to let go of my past. I am totally yours. I was raped when I was a little girl, and it made me a bitter woman. Then I fell in love for the first time, and he was killed two years ago. He saved my life and he saved ALL of the Porters lives. He was a man that I was comparing you to … and I didn't want to let go," she looked away.

"Then you pursued me and I realized you were sent from the man above for me to love. MY trust issues are gone. Don't ever doubt that it is you … and NO ONE else that I love from this day forward!"

He had heard her pour her heart out. He now understood the reason, she reacted like she did. He had never met any woman that could compare to her. She was gentle and kind, but then she could be demanding, and commanding him to be the best lover. It was his pledge to never disappoint her.

He kissed her and they made slow passionate love that built until it overflowed with goodness! He said, "OH Baby I am so in love with you!"

"Good and I will promise to keep it that way," Michelle said.

"I am going to take a bubble bath. Do you want to come?"

"I want to do everything with you! I got a feeling my love that will be my every day mantra. I WANT TO DO EVERY THING WITH YOU!"

They bathed each other and the large marble bathroom with the biggest jacuzzi was theirs. "We picked the best room, most do not have a jacuzzi!" she stated.

"That Trevor sending a bottle of champagne made a difference, too. You were not as uptight after the first glass!" Robert smiled.

"I know it was nice to not have to pretend … just be ourselves. I want you again already!" Michelle said.

"You are kidding?" Robert grinned.

She got on him and he said "Tallyho!" She rode him to the hunt where his prize was caught mid-air.

"You are killing me. I need it all the time now! HOW will I ever be able to hold it together long enough to give a lecture without thinking of you? If I think of you, I will get hard!"

"You take ice cubes and freeze it before hand!" she grinned.

"You are kidding." he swallowed.

"Yes, but I do have a night, I will use ice to arouse my new husband and experiment with things that I have read about. I am well read on sexual positions and dominatrix. Cosmopolitan magazine has been an interesting source this year," she laughed heartily.

He didn't know she was trying to act like a lady and reading some of these cultural mags had only given her more erotic information than was on the streets.

"Do you like to be tied up and feathered, or handcuffed and iced, or licked with chocolate syrup oozing in all the right places?" she was asking to find out his preferences.

"Don't! You are blowing my mind! I want you so badly … look see what you have done this never happened to me before," he gulped.

"You have never had me before!" she said sucking his tits.

"Her Holy Majesty!" boing … boing

Morning was breaking when they finally slept.

She arose at ten and made a pot of coffee and served him.

"We have to go and get a ring and marriage license before Trevor is toting his shotgun. He used to be an excellent shot!"

Robert stated.

She sipped, smiling at him in her birthday suit. No shyness only open and honest trust for him.

"Don't come near me!" he said. She licked her lips and he reached, and pinched her tit that was hard. She sucked on his ear, and kissed his eyes and crawled over him and settled, "Oh, morning delight! Am I too near?"

He was speechless. All he did was moan and moan, and pull her back and forth until neither could stand it. He laid her down and sealed the deal. Yes, it was ridiculous how much they had denied each other in the six months. Now, they were making up for it!

"Cream with your coffee?" he asked.

"Always, my darling!" she answered.

At twelve noon, they were dressed and finally out the door, got the license, married and at nine PM, returned home with a ring on her finger and a smile on both their faces.

They apologized and went to their room and made love until early morning. "How on earth have I lived a day without you?" Robert asked.

"I don't know how I fought it for six months," Michelle said.

"I wanted you so badly at the cafe and in the subway every-one knew!" Robert stared at her, "Truly love, they ALL did!"

To Be Continued

Printed in the United States
By Bookmasters